Oregonism

(Bona Pax Ordinis)

By Fred Sottile

This is a work of fiction. The events and characters described herein are imaginary, and are not intended to refer to specific places or living persons. The opinions expressed in this manuscript are solely the opinions of the author and do not represent opinions or thoughts of the publisher. The author has represented and warranted full ownership and/or legal righto all the materials in this book.

Published by Pro Se Publications

ISBN: 978-0-9897843-4-4

Printed in the United States of America

Other Fiction by

Fred Sottile

American King

National Pastime

Who Art in Heaven

Non-fiction

Murder of a Little Girl

Biography

Hotsy Totsy FemiNazi

Fictionalized Biography

The Caterwaul

Contents

This book is dedicated in loving memory to

Marc Angelucci

Oregonism

(Bona Pax Ordinis)

Chapter One

Rige Coos Bay

"We're not a nation of laws, we're a nation of permission," Orazio said. Orazio Rige had plenty of money from his international shipping business. He was on yet another blind date with a woman whose computer dating-site name was Maya 25, who looked like a pretty good prospect from her profile. As attractive as her picture, and politically conservative, the date should have been going better.

Orazio, "Ratzi," for those who love him, was one of those classic most eligible bachelors. Intelligent, handsome and successful, you'd think he wouldn't need to computer date, but Coos Bay is basically a small town, and Orazio was conspicuous, so had the "right girl" been front and center, his love life would already have been a done deal. Trouble was, the "right girls" were already working for him at the shipping company and he valued them enough to keep his hands off.

Maya 25 was a fine lady, she just had too much "main stream media" in her to move quickly through the clever ideas that Orazio was throwing out to her. First, he wanted to use his money to influence politicians, not for the sake of his business, but for the sake of his philosophy. This alone was hard for politicians, and apparently Maya, to understand. The man had money enough that he would never miss another meal, and enough to keep the wolves from his door. He didn't need more money, but was well able to make more.

So what to do with it? Well, when you hit the lottery, we find out who you really are. If you're going to kill yourself with dope, now you will. If you're going to play golf every day, your whole life becomes anticipation of the next tee time which weather permitting, will be the next day. Go fishing, play the piano, chase women, rescue dogs? We'll meet the real you. Orazio wanted to reform government. He wanted a woman who understood this and was not afraid or overwhelmed. He didn't want her to work on it. He just wanted her to understand him. Maya wanted the rich guy to take her to resorts. Not a match; too bad. Nice lady.

*****

Two of the women already in Orazio's life were Marla and Donna Black. Two sisters, thirty six and thirty five, who were in the same boat as their boss! Knock out good looks, but not a lover between them. Killer accountant-attorney combination, they had devoted their lives to corporate chicanery. They never worked a day in their lives. For them, each day was game on. They considered a court conflict or audit to be fun. They were so involved with the politicians, law enforcement, and judiciary in their State that they were incapable of being surprised. They had thought-through and anticipated every imaginable fall-out from their "moves" and were ready for them. Half the time, they got away with bending the rules because they moved so quickly, that any opposition was just not capable of keeping up. Because of their quirky intensity, some thought that they may have had a little aspergers. Whether that was true or not, in their environment, they were formidable. When tag-teamed in the cross-fire of the "Black Force" in business, you were quickly running for merciful resolution.

Orazio called for a meeting with the Blacks. What worked for him was a sounding board. He thought when he talked. For good or bad, until he was verbalizing his ideas, he had a tough time thinking things through. The Black sisters were perfect for this. They were ruthless.

The boss started the meeting by asking, "Just out of curiosity, how much money do you two have at this point?"

"None of your business, but we know exactly how much you have Ratzi," Donna said.

Marla asked, "Why, do you need an investor?"

"No" Orazio said, "I'm just amazed by why you still work for me when you don't have to."

Donna smirked, "Work? We don't work for you. We work for ourselves. We just hang with you because you give a shit about stuff and we don't. Gotta have a purpose, right? You're our charity-case, tough guy. You asked about our money? Don't worry, we have more than you."

Orazio looked at them; looked at their smiling faces. Did they have more money than he? He'd never know. It was their style to play with your head like that. Leave you unsure. He loved 'em; beautiful in their own way, yet potentially lethal. It was like having a loyal pair of pet tigers.

He brought up the subject. "I had a date last evening with a nice lady…"

Donna interrupted, "Oh no, here we go, dude, why don't just marry Koslowski and be done with the torture?"

Orazio nodded but said, "Carole Koslowski works for me. You know my rules."

Donna said, "Right, so fire her and marry her. For her it's an upgrade. She'll do it. She'd love to spend your money."

"No," Orazio said, "She's a human resources genius, and she loves her job. I'm not going to tempt her away, only to find out that it pulls her heart out. I want her in her office, not my kitchen."

Marla looked stunned, "Kitchen? That would be a terrible waste of good Koslowski. That woman is a bedroom unit. Good in the parlor, good at the pool, with any luck, the nursey, but kitchen? Ratzi, get real. Besides, you consider a real good pizza as one third of a really great day. Kitchen? What kind of fantasy could you possibly have that takes place in a kitchen?"

Again, Orazio loved them. He wondered, what kind of fantasies do they have? Do they even like men? Do they have them? Maybe chained in a basement somewhere? He didn't ask.

4

Orazio said, "Okay, enough about my personal problems. I just mentioned it because of what I had it boiled down to when I was talking in the restaurant. I want to bring up two things. First I want to evolve the election system. I want more accountability. I want easy access to government positions. The election laws are intentionally difficult to comply with and are overseen by nasty bureaucrats who also need a dose of accountability to hold their feet to the fire.

The second thing is I want some STEM kids."

Donna smiled, "Koslowski will make about six of them for you."

Orazio: No, I want them right now. But speaking of Carole Koz, I think I should get her in on this. She's HR. She can find them. I'll talk to her tomorrow, but I want you two to know where I'm going with this.

Marla jumped in, We know where you're going. You have a shipping business. Boats, clerks, longshoremen, and lawyers; it runs itself. You have investment capital. You want an R & D department. You want to research and develop something. Make your mark on the world. You need to fight a Bond Villain, no never mind that. Whatever it is, the government is going to be a problem. You'll need to fix that, probably on the fly. You need us to use our tricks of the trade to grease the skids and run interference while you move forward. Diversionary tactics, litigation logjams, stonewalling, corporate espionage, international intrigue, yeah, we're in.

Orazio: Did she just see a movie?

Donna: Ratzi, she wants to make a movie.

Marla: You've always been a kinda blue collar guy forced into a business suit. You want to surround yourself with techy egg-head guys who've never done a day's work in their lives, but can work all night.

Donna: I think he's more like picturing egg-head girls. What is it? What's the project you want to do? I do like the Bond Villain image. I think you need to pet a big furry cat while you call the shots. I hope you don't think you're Elon Musk or something. You're not as smart and not as creepy. Creepy's not fair. Let's say eclectic? What is it? What's it gonna be?

Orazio: Donna please, I don't know what it is. That's for me to discover when I talk to the STEM kids. They're going to rule the world someday. One of those kids is going to come up with something that will be impossible for government to get their hands on. Something so unimaginable that the regular retards in D.C. won't even have a rudimentary understanding; and the kids who create it will just be an evolutionary step above government. Not necessarily a weapon, although that possibility is considerable. Look, stuff like Amazon and Facebook are world beaters and they are nothing but an online store and a social network device. Can you imagine something real, like inexhaustible food, inexhaustible energy, or even the colonization of space? I want to back something so visionary that at the moment, it's inconceivable. I'm looking for a visionary, a real weird kid with even weirder friends. Get it? It's a quest.

Donna: Koz is the headhunter. Do you want us with you when you bring this to her? We're really going to do this? This is next level stuff. I mean you know; we need this. Our game has become a stacked deck, right Marla? I'm picturing underground labs. Ultra-secret Manhattan Project clearance protocol, like they have to live right on site. Like, we have to make sure the thing doesn't get away from us, like the scientists go rouge somehow. These STEM kids are crazy smart. I mean, if they have what it takes to come up with something revolutionary, they probably have the ability to protect it, like no matter what we do. Fuckin cool.

Orazio: Look let's not start pouring the concrete yet okay. I'm not sure what the project will be. Maybe we can do it above ground okay? But, I do want to venture forth. It's going to take a lot of diligence. I appreciate your enthusiasm. I'm 100% stronger with you than without you. Should we have a drink?

Donna and Marla together, "Johnny Blue."

Chapter Two

Kozlowski

Marsha was a school teacher and a union member. Orazio met her at the gun shop. She was buying an FMK 9mm automatic. She got the one with the pink frame, which Orazio thought was cute. "Self-defense," she said as she saw him looking. "There are going to be a lot of crazies out there soon."

"Wanna go back to the range? I'll buy you some ammo." He said, looking at her fit athletic figure. "Thanks but no," she replied. "Don't know how to use it yet. I've got classes coming up; maybe after I'm not so self-conscious about having a gun in my hand." Orazio asked why she was self-conscious. She said, "I'm a big Lefty politically, I've always been anti-gun." "Yet here you are. What compelled the change of heart," Orazio asked.

The woman told Orazio that she lived in a very upscale neighborhood, but the City Council had decided to put Section 8 housing at the end of her street. Though the whole neighborhood had protested the permission, the project was moving forward. She told Orazio that she was furious because she had considered her house to be an investment, and that the Section 8 housing would bring down her property value.

Orazio listened to her tale of woe. He pointed out to her that the City Council was reflecting her very own philosophy of providing homes so that her neighborhood would be diverse, and that the children of the poor would be going to school with her children, despite the fact that they did not share the Jewish culture that was predominant in her neighborhood. She said that she knew that but she didn't want her philosophy to affect her investment. He told her that she was in conflict. She denied his observation. "I'm not in conflict," she said. "I know exactly what I want. I want to keep my real estate value. I worked hard to buy and maintain this property. It's mine and I don't want the value taken away."

Orazio asked, "So you don't want what you've worked hard for to be taken away so some stranger can have an advantage?" "Right," she raised her voice. Orazio held his hand out for a hand shake and said, "Well Lefty, welcome to the Republican Party."

*****

Carole Kozlowski was to people what the Black sisters were to business. She had an innate skill set that was part training and part intrinsic. She was a real people-person.

First was her warmth. She had an ability to make you think that there was something special going on between you and her. Everybody in the company thought that they had a special understanding between them, just outside the professional relationship. It was something in her face that just said to you, "The fact that you are more special than anyone else knows is known to me, and I know you know I know. We'll just keep my admiration for your qualities to ourselves, you know, just between us." It was bewitching, and was equally embracing for both men and women. It wasn't that she winked at you, because she didn't. It was like she gave you an eighth of a wink; just enough to give you, not hope, but some weird compelling desire to love her for her intimate recognition and appreciation of you.

Next was what she trained for, body language, especially in the face. When Miss Kozlowski looked at you, you were under investigation. As able to read your face and body, she was equally able to mask her own reactions, or use hers to manipulate you. She was a demon at the poker table. Donna and Marla Black marveled at her. They were bludgeon fighters. Koz worked under cover of a smile and a nod. The Blacks forced you to move in the direction they wanted. Carole made you move while thinking it was your own idea. The Blacks considered deeply their ability in combat against her. The battlefield would be incomprehensible to them. They wondered if put up against her, they could prevail. They knew they would never have to find out, because after all, they had a special relationship with her that was "just between them."

Then, there was the professional Human Resources manager that she was by trade. She had an industrial knowledge of what her company needed and was completely aware of what the market was for talent. She knew what competitors were providing in incentives for their humans, and was always ready to make her offer irresistible. Everybody working at Rige Coos Bay was damn glad to have the best job they could ever find. They knew that they were there to stay. Mr. Rige was always quick to develop his employees' aspirations for advancement, so the idea of "out and up" was seldom considered by his people. The company had a credo of "In and Up." Rige Coos Bay had a retention rate for employees that made all of its associates proud. Plus, they had a compelling relationship with that foxy HR lady.

Orazio tried to schedule a meeting with her. She asked what the meeting would be about, and how much time they would need. He told her that he wanted to staff a new division of the company, and that he first needed to bring her to

10

understand the philosophical basis for the direction he wanted the new division to take. Carole recommended a private room in a very exclusive restaurant. Orazio was off balance right away.

Orazio: Carole, why don't we just have it right here in one of our already too many offices?

Carole: No, we need a romantic setting.

Orazio: Look Carole, this is not romance, this is business.

Carole: Oh Ratzi, how wrong you are. This isn't romance between you and me, its romance between you and your half-baked idea. I know you. You want to go off on some ideological trip don't you? You want me to marvel with you. You want me to fall in love with your idea. You want me to give it the enthusiasm that comes from a personal commitment of my own. Am I Right? I do the same shit to people.

Orazio: Dead wrong Kozlowski. This is an atypical situation. This is not something I want you to just dump on your staff. This is something that I want you and you alone to prioritize. You can't pick the people I need without having a heart to heart with me. I need really unique people for this project. I need freaks. I need visionary recruitment. I'm going to ask you to delegate everything else in your department and do this job alone and fulltime.

Carole: My dear Orazio Rige, I love watching you circle me as I circle you. You just supported what I said. Our little power struggle is so romance novel. We're both powerless against each other aren't we? I still dream of working for you, even though I already work for you. You know I'm all-in for you, and I know you're terrified of having me, and equally terrified of losing me. There is business that should be conducted here amongst the chrome and foam of our offices, but this, if we're going to do something memorable, let's start it in a proper setting. If we're not going to end up in bed with each other, let's at least drink and pass out with each other.

Orazio: These are your terms aren't they?

Carole: Terms? Never! It's my desire.

Orazio: Where and when?

Carole: When? The suspense is killing me. Tonight, the Homestead, six o'clock, I'll make the reservation myself. Look, I need to leave right now to get my hair done.

Orazio: Your hair is fine.

Carole: You're an idiot. And wear the dark gray Brioni suit with the light gray tie.

Orazio: Why that?

Carole: Because I only have one dress that goes with the hairstyle I'm going to get, and that suit is the only one you have that goes with that dress.

Orazio: You know I want to ravage you right here on the desk don't you?

Carole: Yes Mr. Rige I do, and I'm sorry, but you should have come here with this sooner because right now I have to get moving.

Orazio turned and left the room while Carole made the reservation call. As he looked back at her he muttered to himself, "I'm doomed."

Out in the hall sitting patiently was Marla Black. She asked matter-of-factly, "Where and when?" Orazio looked at her and just said, "Six o'clock at the Homestead." Marla said back, "Fine, I'll have Bobby do a complete electronic surveillance sweep." Orazio looked at her eyes and said, "Yeah, and please for God's sake don't plant one of your own." Marla feigned shocked surprise and replied, "Little old me, bug you?"

Orazio turned, and as he walked away, muttered again, "I'm doomed."

The Homestead was a masterpiece of architecture. Lodged in a woodland setting, the first thing you noticed was the smell of pine. The approach was pine trees that grew from the natural bed of pine needles. The trees were gardened, and wildlife was attracted. Seeing the well protected deer was common on the way up the quarter mile drive from the gate to the grand entryway. The building itself was a synergy of natural elements enhanced by modern technology. The wood was completely fireproof, and the windows were all double pain for insulation, but looked as if they had risen right up from the ground. The stream running through the property produced enough electricity for the landscaping lights that ran all night long, and for the kitchen refrigeration. Inside, the rooms had each a different character depending on the size and style of your event. For Koslowski plus one, the second floor room had a classic French Colonial table for two, set before a breakfront that held the actual dishes that they would eat from. To the side were a sofa and two wingback chairs that looked out of a balcony window onto the lake that fed the stream below.

A chef prepared his famous Coos Bay seafood dinner, which was served by a waitress who was always on call. Also in the room was a bar with anything you might need for two adults, who were no longer thinking, but respectably drinking like a civilized lady and man. They arrived separately.

Rige was always awe-struck by Carole Kozlowski's beauty. He thought, an undiscovered movie star, she would have had a fan base that was wrapped around her finger. He was glad that he had worn the suit that she had more or less demanded. He was also really glad that he had also gotten a haircut. The staff at the homestead had unrelenting good taste and would have noticed and frowned upon the gentleman's lack of detail in his kit. Of course, never would a word be said, but the discomfort of the missed detail would start the evening off at only ninety-nine percent of the perfection it could be. Orazio did arrive a bit early so as not to keep the lady waiting as she made her entrance from the company limousine, through the front doors and over to the front bar. Her allure was a totally confident display of understated power.

Carole: Orazio, you got a haircut.

Orazio took her hand and just nodded. "I feel as though I let work absorb me to the point that I don't do things like this enough. I really feel good Carole. Thanks for your vision for our evening, and I'm so honored to be in the company of a woman who can turn every head in the place, even the girls." She said back, "Especially the girls."

Robert, the host, awaiting the proper moment for his approach could see them exhale, and the moment arrive. He stepped toward them, smiled and in the most charming way said, "Get it while it's hot." They looked at each other appreciating his moment of slightly indiscrete intimacy with them.

Carole: Why Robert, how slutty of you.

Robert: Why Carole, I could have only meant your dinner.

Orazio: Well we're right back in high school together again aren't we?

Robert: Isn't it great? I'm always so happy to see you.

The three hugged and Robert walked the couple to the elevator. "Oh no," Carole said, "I really want to walk up that staircase." Each gentleman took an arm and the three of them ascended. At the top, Robert introduced Indira who he said would be there for them for the evening. She nodded to the couple, opened the door to their dining room and asked, "Is there anything I can do for you immediately?" Orazio said, "Since were having fish, just bring a bottle of Chenin Blanc; something nice. We're going to be staying late talking so after dinner, a bottle of Argonaut Speculator ought to be enough, after that, we can let you go. Thank you Indira."

They walked directly to the table. There was enough bread and salad already there that in truth, they didn't need the entrée. Orazio pulled out the chair for Carole, and the two of them sat down and just stared at each other. Finally beginning to eat, Orazio, still stunned by Carole said, "Damn it Koz, you're too freakin' distracting. The bite, the swallow, I forgot how I wanted to start this." "Well work your way through it boss, I'm here to listen," she said.

Orazio looked at her and asked himself, how do you go for her, and how on Earth do you not go for her? They had a few appetizers, and gazing at each other, talked about their high school days with their host Robert and his wife Rhonda, and how proud they were that the two had built the Homestead.

As the sizzling entrees arrived, Orazio was delighted enough for the distraction to be able to get back on his mission.

Orazio: Carole, we are on a conversation of discovery. I have some objectives in mind, but people are so conditioned by their upbringings, their paradigms, their presuppositions that I can't find anyone who isn't suffering from paralysis by analysis. Everyone I talk with wants to work within a system that has been designed to protect the people established in some kind of power structure. We have to find people who think outside of that structure. People who just don't care who you are, or who the hell you think you are, or who everybody thinks you are.

Carole: Can you narrow it down, because of how we're starting off here, I think I'm going to have to search many options in different fields. I'm going to look in medical, engineering, philosophical, I mean, my mind is already reeling.

Orazio: No, I can't narrow it down yet. Look, real power comes from ability. It seems that the greatest power in the world today is held by politicians. This is absurd. The reason for this is because it is granted by the world full of followers. We have this goofy voting deal, where real idiots are massed together and we accept the choices made by the vast swaths of people who know virtually nothing.

People don't know a fact from an opinion. I constantly find people saying, "Well, that's your opinion," when I'm stating a fact. I'll give you an example.

There are two identical homes. They're side by side.

One has roses on it; the other has tulips on it.

The fact is, both properties are identical.

If you prefer to be on the one with the roses because you like roses, your opinion is that given the choice, you'd prefer to be on the property with the roses. Your opinion regarding flowers does not affect the fact that the property under both is identical. I actually heard this argument recently.

These nitwits vote. Voting is not real power. Voting is power granted to ignorant, controllable people who aren't even smart enough to understand that they are voting for people who are chosen because there are already compromised.

Someday, a person, or people with real power will come along and the whole system in place will be disregarded. Not overthrown, just disregarded. They won't need it. The problem is, will they be benevolent, or will they be malevolent? We need to find the ones who are benevolent.

Carole: That's why you need me. You want my insight into the personal qualities of the applicants, more than their ability.

Orazio: No, we need both. See, there was a man down in Brazil named Arigo; Arigo, surgeon of the rusty knife. He died back in 71. He lived in the wilds of Brazil near Belo Horizonte. He supposedly conducted surgery in a condemned church in unsanitary conditions with a pocket knife. He spoke another language while doing this. He prescribed drugs only found in other countries and for ailments not intended for those drugs. His success rate was nearly perfect. He even cured the President of his country's wife of inoperable cancer. It's an incredible story. Press came from Europe and America to check out the stories. They pretty much confirmed the whole crazy thing. The guy could only do his miracles in the dilapidated rural church. Anywhere else, he had no idea of how to do much of anything. He was actually a Brazilian social security agent by trade. Oh, and the guy never asked any money for his services. He basically did this stuff on his day off from work.

Now, someday there will be a person capable of something like this who actually knows what he's doing.

Carole: Or she.

Orazio: God, don't give me that politically correct shit, it's toxic to the flow of thought.

Carole: Sorry.

Orazio: Arigo was put in jail for doing medical practice without a license. Hundreds of people were waiting for a miracle, and a bureaucracy was breaking his balls. I think what I'm getting at here is we need to find a genius, develop his potential, and have the Blacks protect him from government.

Now, will it be medical? Maybe.

What if it's engineering? What if we get a guy who creates a free energy source? I don't know how that would be possible. I'm a guy who made a fortune burning diesel, but what if? We'd have to protect the world economy. How, I don't know.

What if it was financial? What if somebody found a way to structure the economy in some new more efficient way? A way that would reward productivity, yet not penalize limited ability, or God forbid, incapacity?

I'm telling you it's the STEM kids: science, technology, engineering and math.

Much as I am committed to this STEM idea, don't rule out theology. There may be a way through faith, but I can't begin to imagine it, but don't rule it out. I just have no idea.

Indira showed up with the Brandy and Orazio asked Indira to bring the chef who prepared their dinner to the room. When they arrive, Orazio gave each one of them a hundred dollar bill and thanked them for sharing their time that evening. Carole told them she was genuine honored by their mission of perfection, and that she and Mr. Rige will find their way out long after closing time. With nothing less than the sincerity of a real culinary artist, the chef said, "Truly wonderful evening for me as well, and thank you." Closing the door behind them, the chef and Indira said in unison, "That lady likes me."

Carole and Orazio moved to the plush parlor sofa, looked out the west watching window at the remaining moments of the summer sunset, talked about people, issues, potential, the future, and sipped the brandy until they both fell asleep.

Chapter Three

Local Government

I was in the parking lot when I noticed a political bumper sticker on a car. I asked the man leaning up against the car if it was his sticker. He said it was. I asked him if he supported the guy whose name was on the sticker. He said he did. I found it hard to believe.

I: But in his first term he didn't make good on any of his promises. Also, he broke laws and promoted policies that hurt the poor.

He: I don't know about all that.

I: Well, it's been in the news for four years. He flipped on all his promises literally from the first day in office.

He: Yeah, well, don't you see that he looks like me? Aren't you gonna vote for the guy who looks like you?

I: Are you saying that you are going to vote simply on race?

He: Yeah, I'm a racist. Aren't you?

I: No, I vote by performance, integrity, you know, results.

He: So you're voting for the guy that looks like you?

I: Well, I mean, I guess I am, but not because we are the same race.

He: Uh, yeah, right, well good luck with your boy. Do you wish me the same?

I: Actually no.

He: Well, that's not very kind. Are you ashamed of yourself for being like that?

I: Actually no. I'm ashamed of you for being a racist.

He: I can be a racist if I want, so can you. I think you need to respect that.

I: Well, I do appreciate your honesty.

He: Well, thank you. First nice thing you said. I'm not saying that you're dishonest, but I do think that maybe you should take a look at your own self before judging others.

I: I'd like to talk more, but actually I'm in a little bit of a hurry.

He: Well then, get yourself along, and good luck with your boy.

I: Okay, thanks, and good luck to you too.

*****

Sex scandal? Kick-back scandal? Nepotism scandal? Salary and pension scandal? We have too much unsupervised government.

So the local election season started. The candidates for everything from School Board to Financial Controllers, to Sheriff began the process of application. Signatures were gathered and fees were paid. People got on the ballot. Why signatures? Why fees? We have tons of already paid clerks. There is already a Registrar of Voters. There are already election officials. Why can't you simply write a postcard and mail it to the Registrar? If you're nobody, you won't get any votes anyway. So why can't your name be on a ballot? If you want to be truly democratic, shouldn't everyone at that point have an equal opportunity? It would be a true gesture for equality, and would cost virtually nothing, so why not?

Next, the promises started. When elected, I will:

Help the poor
Create jobs
Address the need for health care reform
Clean up the environment
Lower taxes on the poor
Raise taxes on the wealthy
Fix the roads and bridges
Empower the underserved minorities
Never deny a woman's right to choose
Work for gender equality for all 56 genders
Close the gender wage gap
Education, you know, for the children
Lower the crime rate
Never forget the Veterans
And most of all, give plenty of FREE STUFF

Rige asked his secretary,

"Did anyone say anything about reducing the size of government?"
"No, Mr. Rige, they didn't."
"Did any of them mention how they were going to do any of this?"
"No Mr. Rige, I don't believe they did."

Orazio Rige began to lay out his plan to win an election. First, he selected a great guy who had no delusions of grandeur, no big ego. The problem with most candidates is they think that people will want to vote for THEM. No one cares about that person. People care about promises and tribalism. Ratzi wants to flip the game. His candidate gets the idea right away. The game is not to have a virtually irrelevant win in an irrelevant place. The game is to restructure the way people see the process. Make the people look at something so different that they engage out of curiosity; in short, give 'em an eye-opener.

The candidate does not have to fund-raise because his campaign is fully run by volunteers. Where is this wonderful army of volunteers? They work at Rige Coos Bay. One thing Rige Coos Bay employees know is that if you help Rige, Rige will never forget.

Ashton Mathews, "Matty" was Orazio's closest friend in high school, a humble guy who was a lineman on the football team who protected Ratzi when he ran the ball. Matty had become a welder in the army and had his twenty years in. He was thinking of a new career anyway, and was excited to do something crazy with his old friend. Matty and Ratzi back in the huddle. Matty was given the new game plan.

Ratzi wanted Matty to take the House of Representative seat. So this is what they did.

Matty produced a list of promises that he presented in writing with his signature.
He promised that he would never vote to:

Raise Taxes
Support New or Increased Fees or Licensing
Support Bond Issuance
Restrict Gun and Ammunition Rights
Expand Government
Raise Salary or Retirement Benefits for Government Employees
Create Special Rights or Privileges for any Special Interest Group
Use Tax Money to "Bailout" a Bank or Business
Allow Sanctuary for Criminals

Or anything else that was just a great big Waste of Money

The declaration also went on to state that if he did vote in violation of his written oath, that betrayal would be cause for his immediate resignation, and forfeiture of any money or other remuneration accepted as compensation for his services while in office. He would put his compensation in a trust account for each term so that it would be immediately available should he renege. Further, the contract would be renewable every two years until such time of his eventual resignation.

He couldn't promise to DO anything, but knew he could certainly promise not to do anything bad. He realized that his campaign would be a threat to the existing power structure, but promised the voters that if they voted for him as an example of what COULD be, others would be compelled to use his campaign as a template for their own success. It was simple. Do you want to take care of people and have the job, or do you want to be an asshole and lose?

It used to be; you could be an asshole and win. The *Matty Contract* would pretty much guarantee improvement. Do you want to be governed by assholes again and again, every friggin time? Now you don't have to be cheated. Matty's Slogan:

Matty for House of Representatives; you finally got it in writing.

*****

Next, Orazio tried another tactic.

In the overlapping State Senate District, there was a woman who voted in favor of a proposition that allowed criminals who committed a crime with a cash value of less than nine hundred and fifty dollars to be **not arrested**, but given a summons to appear in court at their own recognizance. Furthermore, a crime such as this could be committed any number of times with no cumulative consequences. Such crimes would only be considered misdemeanors; nothing much worse than a traffic ticket. And to top it off, criminals already in prison for such crimes would have their judgment reduced, and would be released.

This State Senate District had two major concerns, safety from crime, and better schools. This Proposition was actually called *The Safe Neighborhood and Schools Act.* Everybody got screwed. Not only did the woman vote for this act but when crime increased dramatically in that district, she did nothing to repeal it. She was one of those assholes we had identified.

The tactic to remove her was revolutionary. The district was about forty percent Asian, forty percent Hispanic and fifteen percent White and five percent Black.

Orazio got three women to run, again, women with no selfishness or flaming ego. An Asian woman, an Hispanic woman, and a Black woman. The three women campaigned together. The three women glorified each other. The three women all had the same message.

All three of us are good choices. Any of us will serve you well. Pick one of us, but whatever you do, DON'T VOTE FOR THE INCUMBENT. We all know that she's bad.

The message was so strong that they knocked the incumbent off in the primary. It went just as expected. The voters went thirty five percent for the Asian Lady, thirty five percent for the Hispanic Lady, fifteen percent for the Black Lady and fifteen percent for the incumbent.

The Asian Tribe voted.

The Hispanic Tribe voted.

The Black and White Tribe voted.

And the Political Party with its Union Members Tribe voted.

The Party that had once held the seat considered it financially wasteful to put up a fight. They conceded. In the actual election, the winning lady simply hired the other two declaring that they were every bit as great as was understood, and that the voters were best off with the three of them working as they had promised. Why waste good leaders that the whole district acknowledged? The voters got to have them all in an amazing display of cooperation and recognition. Really, no voter was a loser.

*****

Back to the House of Representative race, the issue of the *Safe Neighborhood and Schools Act* hit the incumbent House Member hard too. He had voted for it as well. He was questioned as to why he wasn't working to repeal it. The prison releases had brought not just an increase in crime, but an increase in homelessness. It was a real problem. Plus he would not sign the *Matty Contract.* It seemed that the Public Employee Workers Union had contributed so much to his campaign that it was now in the spotlight as a scandal.

Ashton Mathews III, Matty, won in a landslide. At the swearing in, people teased him about his name, Ashton Mathews the Third. They said it sounded kinda pretentious, especially for a humble Black Dude like Matty. He always said back, "Right. It doesn't really sound right without the SIR in front of it.

So it was that a school teacher named Aimee Tzu, and a retired Army welder named Sir Ashton Mathews the Third came to represent local politics in Orazio Rige's district.

Chapter Four

The Store

For Orazio Rige, the idea came right out of nowhere. A young man named Ryan Chang scheduled an appointment with him. Who he was and what the meeting was for, he did not know. Mr. Chang had an interesting idea.

Chang: Good morning Mr. Rige. My name is Ryan Chang. I work in your accounting department. I had an employee review the other day and the lady who talked with me asked me to talk with Miss Kozlowski.

Rige: Was it a pleasure?

Chang: Wow, what a weird question? But actually, yes it was. I mean, I actually remember thinking it was. She made me think that talking with you was in your best interest instead of mine. I felt strong. She said that you were a good partner. I got excited.

Rige: I like excited. Whatta' ya got?

Chang: We pay a lot of money in taxes. That's my department. Payroll taxes, income taxes, and sales taxes. What I propose is this. Open a great big store, kinda like Costco. Costco has a membership. We don't need that because we have a better identifier.

We have our own coins for the store. Vegas has chips. We're not coining money. That would be illegal. Coined money in America is supposed to be backed by gold, but it no longer is. It's backed by the faith and credit of America. We're okay with that because America probably isn't going out of business any time soon. Rige Coos Bay probably isn't going out of business any time soon. See?

Now, we give each employee a pay cut of say $100 a week. Instead we give them our coins. It works because we have an exchange office. NOT a Bank, where they can exchange their coins for American money.

Most won't, because the coins will be worth, let's say, a dollar twenty on the dollar at the store. This works because the store is non-profit. All it has to do is make its expenses. The benefit to us is tax savings. See?

Now, the store is fine for starters, but eventually, the coins could be used for other commodities. Fuel comes to mind immediately. See?

Rige: And more tax savings.

Chang: Right. Now the idea gets heady. Because the coins are basically an exchange media, not a creation of debt like the fractal monetary system that our government has in place. There will be no inflation. The coins will never lose value. In fact, as American currency loses value, the exchange rate will change in our favor as a natural occurrence. Our coins will be worth more as time goes by, not less like American currency. See?

Here's the difference. In our country's fractal money system, money is created out of thin air. We don't do this.

Look at it this way. Money is based on a commodity or service. A farmer has 100 bushels of wheat. The Federal Reserve creates $100 to represent the value of America's new asset so it can be exchanged. Each bushel becomes worth one dollar. Cool. Now, we eat the wheat, but the cash stays in circulation. Not cool. Next year, we get another 100 bushels so the Fed creates another $100 to represent our new asset. But we no longer have the old asset. We ate it, but the old cash stays in circulation, so now we have 100 bushels, but 200 bucks. Now you need two bucks to buy a bushel. That's inflation. We don't do that.

It's even easier to understand with a service. A guy waxes your car. You give him $100. You don't create a fake $100 to represent his service, but the government does. The waxed car drives off and the transaction is done. After a while, the wax is gone, but the cash lives on. With the debt instrument of American cash, the cash representing his work actually devalues the value of everybody's work from that day on. It's crazy, but it's true.

We give our employee our 100 coins, and she spends them at our store. I say she because women do 85 to 90% of the purchasing in America. Women will love this. Everything is 20% off, see?

The store goes back to us to get the $100 that we didn't give her in her pay. That's how we have the money, and that's how the store gets paid. When the store gives us the "fake" coins, we destroy them. The commodity is gone; the money representing it is gone. No inflation occurs. See?

I'm honest enough to call our exchange currency "fake money." The American government, whose money is even more fake isn't honest enough to own up to their scam. Theirs's is a fake taxation scam, ours is an Even-Steven honest exchange instrument.

It's the tax or interest that inflates the money. We don't contribute to that. Actually, what we're doing is patriotic, if you want to be honest. We're helping Americans retain the value of their cash.

Our money is an exchange instrument, not a debt instrument. I know it's a lot to swallow at once. Miss Kozlowski said you were sharp and not to underestimate you and it's hard for me to sugar-coat shit, stuff, things. I have a problem with overestimating people's cognitive ability so I apologize if my tone seems a little arrogant or aggressive. I guess I'm a little socially awkward, but I mean well. If I'm upsetting your sensitivity, please give me some slack. I'm a smart speaker, but not a nice speaker.

Rige: No, you're doing fine. I'll be kind to myself too and say maybe I'm a little too direct sometime. We're both okay. Let me have it.

Chang: As I said, the store is just the beginning. There are other benefits, accounting benefits that come with having essentially your own bartering tool. The outside world, that is people not from our company, will covet our coins. As we begin to create other stuff for sale, we will avoid sales tax because we are not using internal revenue money. Our products and services will be ten percent cheaper for that reason alone. Am I stating the obvious? Am I wearing out my welcome?

Rige: No, no, I'm very happy to have a visionary like you working for me.

Chang: Oh, that's disappointing. I don't consider myself working for you. I consider myself working with you. In fact, I want the store. I want to run it. I want to eventually run the whole monetary system that I intend to create. Miss Kozlowski seemed to think that you would be open to this and that I could speak frankly. Really, it's kinda the only way I can. Was I wrong to bring this to you this way? I have respect issues.

Rige: No, not at all. Miss Kozlowski is right. You've presented yourself well, but it seems that you may be afraid that I will steal your idea, and worse, not give you credit. Well, to reassure you, that can't happen. Once you told Miss

Kozlowski the idea, you in essence, had copy-written it. In your spirit of working WITH me, you can understand that Miss Kozlowski works WITH me too. See?

Chang: You said see. Are you making fun of me?

Rige: No, bonding. Now you're in trouble Ryan. Now That you've committed to an agreement between us, you have to make this work.

Chang: Work? Don't worry. This is a game I've wanted to play since junior high. You do realize the money will be on a card, not an actual coin right?

Rige: I'm leaving it all up to you until I have a problem. It seems that you can handle problems, and realize that if I have one, I'm still on your side. Also, not all ventures succeed so I don't demand success, but in your case, I'd be surprised if this thing didn't blast off.

Make an appointment with Deanna to see me once a week. Also have HR replace you at your day job. You know, the one you had back when you worked for me. You will get the same pay plus $100 worth of the new …….. we're not calling it The Chang …. and not The Rige …. So ..

Chang: No, nothing like that. Whatta you wanna be, some kind of egomaniacal despot? It's the X, you know, for exchange. And it's decimal. 1X, 10X 20X, and the small fragments are called change. So something will be 1X 25 Change; a buck and a quarter. Simple. See?

It was starting. Kozlowski was doing her job. Ratzi wondered what would be next.

Chapter Five

The Massachusetts Guys

Rod Rodriguez, Mitch Roggenbuck and Dana Morea originally got together to play pinochle. They had Lynette Cowles at that time too, but had to get rid of her because she was too disagreeable. Why they mentioned Lynette, I never did find out.

Also at the meeting were Marla and Donna Black, who brought a suitcase, a laptop, and two separate recording devises.

Rod, Mitch and Dana flew in from Massachusetts. Unannounced, Rod brought his younger brother Oscar from Los Angeles, who buy looking at his hands, you could tell that he was a laborer of some kind. Cuts and burns with the kind of engrained dirt that could never be removed with soap and water.

Orazio was struck to see that they all had backpacks. The backpacks were actually their carryon luggage. He said to himself that it was the first time he had seen someone bring their carryon luggage to this kind of meeting. To him it just looked unprofessional, but he had asked for this, so, okay.

They were dressed in flannel and kakis with hair that looked like they had two separate haircuts on the same heads. With ink in their skin and piercings through their flesh, Orazio could only conclude, these kids hate skin. They were all from families who had money, but clearly they had no respect for anything financial. They just wanted to play. Again, Carole was finding the kind of people we were looking for. They brought no resumes. It wasn't that they were arrogant; really, it seemed that they were oblivious to how easily it would be for a businessman to dismiss them. They styled themselves as backyard engineers with a slant toward ecology; entrepreneurs with 100% confidence, 0% resources, victims of a profit based society. Blah, blah blah.

Rige's feeling was that they had been hanging out together kinda way too long, reinforcing their own egos. Now he would be stuck for way too long. Carole scheduled the whole day for them. He took a naproxen and went in to the meeting; shook hands with Rod, Oscar, and Mitch, Dana looked at my hand and said, "I don't do that."

Orazio introduced the Black sisters who looked at Dana, held back their hands and said, "We don't do that either Honey."

Mitch started off by standing.

Mitch: Mr. Rige, we have a multi-level proposition for you. If you have the patience to follow the vision through to the end, you won't be able to say no. We have a demand for energy in this country. I think we can agree on that. The problem is the "energy" companies. What we are proposing is not revolutionary or innovative at all. In fact, it already exists here on a very small scale. We need to bump that up. The reason that we come to you is that you can create a closed environment. In other words, you can supply your own energy without disturbing the rest of the world. We go under the radar to some degree, but we set the example. We want people to see your success and demand it for themselves.

What we want you to build is a geo-thermal electric plant. It's all upside. Even by Dana's standard.

The pros are:
Virtually Zero Pollution, right Dana
It is virtually impossible to exhaust a geo-thermal reservoir once it is established
Inexhaustible potential
Not variable like wind or sun. Always consistently ON

No fuel
Can be built mostly underground, so landscape is unaffected,
right Dana

The cons have been considered and addressed:
Can cause earthquakes. No problem. We have selected
Prineville, a geologically stable area.
Not cheap to start. No Problem. You clearly have the money.
Water is needed to run the turbines. No Problem. We have the
Pacific Ocean.

Dana stood up.

Dana: Prineville is an arid area that was founded on logging.
Its rainfall is about ten inches per year, mostly in the winter.
The idea would be to bring a biodegradable iron pipe from the
Pacific Ocean near a right-of-way along highway 126, from
Florence. We'll have to bypass Eugene to the south but
reconnect with the 126 past the Bob Straub Parkway
somewhere and then it's right out north of Bend directly to
Prineville.

Turbines run on steam. Steam is distilled water. Free
desalinated water. I intend to build a lake of clean water and
irrigate the entire area. That arid region will become a garden.
Today Oregon, tomorrow Nevada! Free clean water on the
other side of the Cascades. We can do it. It will pay for itself.
It's all upside, agricultural job creation, economic prosperity
and completely sustainable.

Orazio: Won't pumping the water be costly?

Dana: We're pumping from the ocean. Tidal pressure pumps
will push it over the Cascades every day with almost no
moving parts. Once on the downside of the mountains, a
siphon effect will take place to draw water from the ocean at
all hours, reducing the strain on the ocean level pumps. That
water will be held in a pool proportioned in size to the need.

The altitude will provide plenty of natural pressure so pumps will not be needed to supply the underground turbines. It will simply pour in. Even maintenance will be simple. The worst thing that can happen is an obviously non-toxic water leak. Even if we abandoned the project, the pipeline would just harmlessly rust away. If I had the damn money, we'd already be doing this. The only question open now is can you get the right-of-way?

Marla Black: That's what we do Honey. Consider it done.

Dana: Why does she call me Honey?

Orazio: She likes you.

And I hope you like her, because if you want your pipe, if you do, you better just about love her, and her little sister too. We're real-world hard-asses here. You want to play in our league; you better put on your big girl pants. Can you do that, or do you need to go to the little girl's room?

Dana sat down, and with a small embarrassed smile, nodded. "Got it," she said, and swallowed.

Donna Black walked over and gave her a cool bottle of water for her drying throat and said, "Cleaned it myself."

Now Rod Rodriguez stood up.

Rod: There is a periodic table of elements. I'm sure you all know that. In your childhood you probably made a battery using a lemon and a potato. That discovery was followed by innovation. Batteries with copper, lead acid like in old cars, zinc, and up the periodic table until now commonly we have the Lithium Ion battery, like in your phone. Lithium is element number three on the periodic table. Lithium Ion batteries far out perform any other kind of battery. Tesla has the Lithium

Ion battery. Without this technology, electric cars would not be practical.

What I have developed is the Helium Ion battery. Element number two on the periodic table. You see the upward progress on the atomic chain? We're there. This battery is so superior to the lithium battery that it will revolutionize the world. Imagine going from here to New York on one charge. If I tried to produce or patent this technology, I fear that I would be killed. It's good that you and your associates are hard-asses because if you want what I got, you're going to have to be. We picture you using our invention in your world without fanfare. Get it going. Run your whole plant using Mitch's geo-thermal, and charge my batteries with it. Mitch is an electrical engineer, Dana is an ecologist, I'm a Chemist, and my brother here, Oscar is a hot-rodder. Let 'em have it *mijo*, this is your shot.

Oscar: Hi guys. Do you like Chevys? I mean, do remember the Chevelle? It was a car that you could get as a:
Two door
Four door
Station Wagon
Convertible
And even a mini pickup truck as the El Camino, remember?
Different size engines, one for economy, a few for more and even more performance.
One platform, every kind of car.

What I have is the Toad.
We build an electric car platform. Since you need about a third of the batteries that a Tesla has, you save a ton of weight and cost, and you have more design flexibility for weight distribution. You want the same weight on all four wheels for optimum braking and cornering. You want rear drive because you have front steering. You don't want a wheel and tire doing three tasks. Fronts steer and brake. Rears drive and brake. It's the best way.

The frame is a simple ladder frame, just like a Chevelle. It's best because you don't have to engineer some complex monocoque chassis. It's best because its adaptability is beyond simple, and we're going to keep this super simple. That's the key.

Next is the cowl. If you don't know what that is, that's the name for the part that holds the dashboard and the front doors. It's the part that the windshield sits on. It's really the heart of the car's body. The cowl stays the same for all the car models. This is done for economy, and what we are making here is an insanely economic platform with sky's-the-limit options. But I'm getting ahead of myself.

Once you have the frame and the cowl, everything else is just an easy option.
So the company, Toad, builds the frame, the cowl, puts in the motor, and places the batteries for optimal weight distribution. That's all cheap and easy. If you want to make the frame longer or shorter, you can, just tell the factory. Same goes for wider or narrower.

So now you have your Toad for say ten grand, but you don't have a body or seats. The basic six styles are available. Two door, four door, convertible, light pickup, station wagon, and minivan. You pick your body for the standard frame. Next is the gut, the interior. There is an appropriate interior for the body style you've chosen, in maybe three colors.

Now you're up to twenty grand. It's a really cheap, really standard, really dependable car for transportation. We keep it cheap by making it exactly the same for decades. Some people just need transportation from a car, and nothing more, but some people need more.

For those people, people like me, we have options. Now Toad will get the ball rolling on this with custom shop upgrades, and that's fine, but the real hot shit will come from the aftermarket, that's what I want. Because the Toad is so standard, innovators everywhere will start to make parts for the car. The ultimate will be a shortened and narrowed frame for a two seat sports car. But I'm getting ahead of myself again, but I am gonna make that. Believe me.

As soon as the car comes out, some guy is going to make a custom hood with a big scoop in it. Next it will be grills, or different fenders with different lights. Then some upholstery shop will make the leather interior, and the removable hard top for the convertible, and the slide out camper tent for the minivan.

You see, a whole industry will develop out of your car, the simple Toad. Used ones will be gold for customizers. Crazy backyard builders will make entire bodies out of exotic materials. Probably right away a mechanic will bolt in a bigger motor. Shocks, suspension, four wheel drive, go crazy. You have to make it easily adaptable so regular people can go crazy. That's the key. I have a million ideas about what I want to do with this. The entry level on this will be what makes the Toad go viral. The potential is what makes it bring the American car culture come back like it once was.

These pictures are an artist rendering of the Toad. You see every style of car, even a minivan which the Chevelle platform never had. Remember, there's no big gas motor and transmission. Every car in these pictures is really the same car with different trim. The Toad is going to be the greatest car of all time. We're talking culture and history here. People will live and die building and rebuilding the Toad. Somebody has to be smart enough to do this. It may as well be you.

Donna Black: Oscar, a car company is a huge startup. Do you have any idea what is involved?

Oscar: Not this one. You give me and my homies two hundred and fifty thousand square feet out by Mitch's power plant and we'll move in with our families and start building the cars for you one by one. We all want this. The plans are complete. We know how to do every part of it. We'll live there and do our thing seven days a week. What the hell else can we do way out there? We will send our kids to school in Bend. It'll work. There's twelve of us in the club. Fifteen bucks an hour to start and give us a dedicated accountant to sign the checks for our shop supplies, tools and materials. Buy a lot of land Hombre. We're gonna need it, and it's gonna go up in value.

Build the power plant. Build the battery, and we'll build the Toad, and a legend. Be sure to take a picture on day one. For us, it's our legacy, our *Vida*. Ready to stand up?

Rod Rodriguez nodded, and Oscar sat down.

Marla Black asked, "Can Donna and I take everybody to lunch?" Everybody nodded. Marla opened the suitcase and said into it, "Please bring me the 15 passenger executive van, were going to the Seven Devils Brewing Company for lunch right away." She turned to Orazio and said, "Ratzi, invite Koz." Dana Morea leaned in to Marla and said, "I'm a Vegan, will I be okay?" Marla summoned up a warm smile and said, "Didn't you hear Mr. Rige tell you I liked you? I picked the place because it is vegetarian friendly. I'm doing my best kid. I won't let you starve." Dana asked, "How did you know I was a Vegan?" Marla gave her half an eye-roll and said, "It figured."

Orazio looked at the crew. He said, "After lunch I'm going to want an hour with each of you individually. Is there any reason that any of you have to return home immediately?" They all said no. Orazio asked if their hotel was okay. They all said yes. He said, "Okay, let's eat, let's talk, let's sleep tonight, and tomorrow, hopefully, we plan.

Chapter Six

The Contract

Rige Coos Bay continued its role of landing cargo and seafood in the port of Coos Bay, but everyone in the company begins to realize that there is more going on than shipping. Realtors are talking. Rige is buying real estate all throughout Oregon. His big box store was noticed by other big box stores in a radius of twenty miles. The demand for his "company money" which is the only currency his stores accept is growing. He is hiring security people and developing security software. All of this is being done without the usual inclusion of politicians. When licensing or land use variances are needed, Rige walks away from the deal. His demand for cooperation is not coercive. He doesn't bully anyone. He simply won't allow bureaucrats to mess with him. His credo in this regard is,

Leave me alone, **or** I'll leave you alone.
Do you want to be left out?

The Black sisters fly a Gadsden flag, "Don't Tread on Me," outside of their office. If you come after Rige, the Black sisters "Cointelpro" machine is turned on. You become investigated and surveilled. Their aggression and quality of work is masked through layers of their own security. No bureaucrat who's used to scared compliance from the general public is up to facing them. It's true even for judges. The ladies are just impossible to be put on defense. Marla and Donna Black are not sadistic. They don't set out to do harm, simply to ensure their team mates are left alone. Active as they were in Rige's business, they moved back to their parent's home in Virginia "to take care of them," but seemed to be doing an inordinate amount of international travel.

Even the power plant licensing went smoothly. Oregon is full of "Political Leftys," and Dana Morea really spoke their language. She rallied the whole state to support the ecologically correct renewable source of alternate energy. Engineering wise, she really did her homework. Mitch schooled her well, and she had all the answers. Much more than that, she was a hero of the liberal people. They liked to identify with her. She was regarded as a stewardess of the land, promising to keep watch over Rige with his 1%er status. He exalted her too. He showed respect, which went a long way to keep his "public interest image" humble.

Oscar Rodriguez turned out to have far more talent than met the eye. First, he and his friends began showing their Chevys in local car shows. Rige had no idea this would happen. But it was great. When his shop was inspected, hell, it was a car shop. There were American cars all over the place. It looked just fine, and, he and his friends were always quick to help the small local community, such as it was. They did things like rescue motorists stranded way out there on the lonely highway and help them without asking for a dime. Orazio Rige couldn't believe it.

Deanna Segal (DS) was the real name of Orazio's secretary. Privately he called her Della because she reminded him of Della Street (DS). She even looked like Barbara Hale with her shoulder padded suits and nineteen fifty's makeup. She was another high school classmate with him, but at that time, she was the rich one and he was just Ratzi, a guy not in her league. She still had her high class bearing and carried it well. She also had the credentials of a full legal secretary, so she worked well with the Black sisters. She was street smart from sports in college; plenty of hard knocks. Her husband was an Oncologist who worked a seventy hour week, so she consumed her time with civic projects as well as her job. Some said that she ran the company. She didn't, but Orazio was well able to take time away with no fear of having no one at the tiller.

One day she brought Ratzi a flyer for a Memorial Day event in Bend. The flyer featured a Los Lobos tribute band with *Watch the Wolf,* the band's name, in italics. Deanne asked, "Aren't the guys in this band in your car company?" And so they were. Orazio looked up at her and laughed out loud. He said, "I love these guys."

*****

It had been well over a year since Matty and Aimee Tzu had been elected to office. Now the next election season was beginning to take shape. Orazio's imagination was in high gear on how to cut corruption and reduce the size of government that was controlling the economic trajectory of a State that he was increasingly beginning to think of as his own.

He had a strong-hold in Coos Bay with Matty and Aimee. He needed to expand that, and create a corridor out to his holdings around Bend. His strategy was simple. He would back any challenger to an incumbent who would sign the "Matty Pledge."

The pledge again was to promise not to:

Raise Taxes
Support New or Increased Fees or Licensing
Support Bond Issuance
Restrict Gun and Ammunition Rights
Expand Government
Raise Salary or Retirement Benefits for Government Employees
Create Special Rights or Privileges for any Special Interest Group
Use Tax Money to "Bailout" a Bank or Business

Allow Sanctuary for Criminals

Or anything else that was just a great big Waste of Money

The beauty of the pledge was that you didn't promise to do anything, you simply promised not to do anything bad. The people understood this. It was put to them very simply. The pledge of course, was impossible for any incumbent to sign. After all, it was their job to support the expansion of government. For the first time, the battle-line was clear.

Orazio conceded the Portland and Salem area. He knew he was not yet in a position to fight there. He knew that he had to slowly develop an image as a philosophical leader who appealed to the heart, not a family legacy leader who promised "free stuff" for the lazy from the financial elite. To do this, his philosophy needed to be clarified. It needed to be made to appeal to people's pride in their "better nature." He needed to make people proud to be an integral part of an even more proud community, not some slob who sucked off of it.

Other than the Portland area, he managed to get people who had a rudimentary understanding that he was going to make the State rich through productivity. The politicians in Salem had a tough time with this, but the people there didn't. Salem, the State Capitol was certainly not "under siege," but it was in a state of heightened surveillance. Citizens were watching. Any incumbents were pretty much hamstrung as far as screwing the public was concerned. Matty had made a name for himself by exposing "pork" in legislation. His rallies and writing always concerned "stuff" in the legislation that was not indicated in the title of the legislation. He was a tenacious reader. He would read the legislation and ask why "weird stuff" was in it. He would literally ask the politician who sponsored the legislation why he was hiding unannounced consequences to legislation that sounded like, and should have been beneficial, but with the stuff, would be bad. He'd say, "Hey, I'm just an old Army welder who doesn't like this. I don't think other people like this. You should know that. Why don't you? I'll bet you didn't ask anybody. I did. The consensus is, and I quote Pastor Peterson, 'Ain't nobody wants this.'" "I'm gonna vote NO." he'd say, and the majority would go right along with him.

The Matty Pledge was working. Orazio Rige realized that to break down the State's philosophy, he would have to draw up a new Constitution. First he would have to make it clear to the people of Oregon what the heck a "Constitution" is anyway; so few know.

"The Constitution" should not be called the Constitution. It should be called YOUR CONSTITUTION, because that's what it is. Most law is created to control YOU. The Constitution, whether State or Federal is just the opposite. It's not a law to control you. It's a contract, an agreement BETWEEN you and YOUR government. Every organism by nature has a right to try to live. That's why they call it life. The opposite of life is not death. The opposite of life is inanimate. A rock is not alive, but it is not dead. It is inanimate. Every organism has a right to defend itself. If you don't have this intrinsic right, you are no better than a rock.

A government is not a natural phenomenon. It is the creation of a tribe. Its purpose is to protect the tribe, not rule it. For ruling, we have tyrants. A government is supposed to protect you from tyranny, not create it.

YOUR Constitution is an agreement between you, an independent walking thinking man or woman, other people like you, and the organization that the bunch of you have created FOR THE COMMON GOOD. The United States Constitution is designed by people who identified tyranny, didn't like it, and proposed an agreement that would protect them from it. IT IS A PHILOSOPHICAL DOCUMENT and LEGAL CONTRACT. It expresses the revulsion we have toward tyranny. Its guarantees are supreme over any argument

44

between you and YOUR government in a court; PERIOD. Any politician who threatens your protection should immediately be identified and recalled, or at minimum, be voted out of office before his/her malevolence is allowed to fester. Everyone should understand this, and agreement with this should be understood at the limbic system level. In other words, even a lizard knows what's in or not in its own best interest. You should be at least that smart.

Orazio set out to make his philosophy known. He knew that he could never just say, "Here it is, adopt it." No. He would have to show everyone the benefits of a philosophical change from fractal money debt based, profit based, consumption based economy, to an ever growing productivity based economy that would leave no one behind. A system designed to bring out the best in everybody. Our current monetary system is based on greed because it is designed by insecure tyrants. Take away the insecurity, and you have no need for greed. The truth is, you are "closer to God" when you realize that absolutely enough, plus one, is one too much. If you don't get it, think of it this way. Go ahead and over eat until you feel bad. That's bad. You would have been better off if you stopped when you had had enough wouldn't you? You would feel good now if you'd been prudent wouldn't you? Feeling good is good. So .... Adopt a philosophy of don't over eat in every aspect of your life and *voila* you'll always feel good. Got it? Basically it's:

Don't push yourself to consume, push yourself to produce.
You'll be exultant and proud of yourself, not, never
unsatisfied and kinda queasy.

Orazio decided a good place to start was with the Constitution we already have. Not the Federal one, that's already perfect, no, the State Constitution. The first thing he noticed was, it was not a people's document. It was written in mumbo jumbo. Perfect example, Article II. Suffrage and Elections. Get the hell out of here. Suffrage? Just say Voting

45

and Elections. Okay, suffrage is a word from the Latin word *suffragium* used seven hundred years ago that actually meant prayer. Like, you pray for something which could also in the context of the time mean vote for something, because let's face it, back then not having a vote was kinda the same as not having a prayer. Basically, you weren't getting something by voting or praying. There were Kings. No voting.

Six hundred years later, the wealthy wanted women to vote so that they, the wealthy, could put equality upon them so they could justify an equal responsibility to freakin work outside the home in their factories. The concept would provide a flood of already housed cheap labor. You know, industrial revolution and all that. Now in our time, women seem to think it's wise to demand to fight and die in combat, looks like they'll fall for anything. Oh well. Soon they'll demand equal suicide rates with men. Seems unlikely but oh those wacky FemiNazis. They're just not happy until every woman is as unhappy as they.

For some reason, in a wild display of arrogance, they called their movement toward the right to vote, the Women's Suffrage Movement. Why? Why not the Women's Voting Rights Movement? Why incorporate, (Did I say incorporate? Sorry.) Why not USE plain English? Why a weird antique language that has no articles. It's just idiotic.

What it is, is written proof that lawyers, judges and legislators are pompous pricks.

Orazio knew he'd have to start from scratch. He decided to jot down a few notes as to issues important to him, and grow the list as ideas presented themselves.

1) English only (in unity is strength)
2) No other cultural icons are accepted (signs must be in English)(no diversity parades)

3) Education is focused on problem solving and team work based on leadership.
4) American citizenship or sponsorship would be a requirement for residency.
5) Judges, police and teachers will be **self-sanitizing.**
6) Judges, police and teachers will be routinely brought before citizen review boards.
7) Protection of intellectual property

He figured that he would evaluate the existing constitution as a starting point and tweak it for a commonsense upgrade.

Preamble

We the people of the State of Oregon to the end that Justice be established, order maintained, and liberty perpetuated, do ordain this Constitution.

That's fine, but ordain? What the hell does ordain mean? It means with priestly authority. Let's just change that to "agree on."

We the people of the State of Oregon to the end that Justice be established, order maintained, and liberty perpetuated, do <u>agree on</u> this Constitution. That's better. Okay here goes.

Article I
Bill of Rights

Section 1. Natural Rights Inherent in People. Everyone has a natural and equal right to work toward changing the government to suit their concept of a more perfect society.

47

Section 2. Freedom of Worship. Worship any way you want. Just respect that everyone else can worship any way they want. The State cannot institute a State Religion. (Islam by its dictates becomes Illegal) I hope you understand this.

Section 3. Manner of Administering Oath or Affirmation. If you swear to tell the truth or pledge an oath on your honor, and you don't tell the truth or violate that oath, that violation will be registered, and you will no longer be allowed to enter into a legal agreement from that day forward.

Section 4. Freedom of Speech and Media. No law shall be passed restraining the free expression of fact or opinion on any subject. Every person shall be responsible for the consequences stemming from the abuse of that right.

Section 5. Common Language All public speech, media and signage will be conducted in the common language of American English so as to unify society and not exclude citizens born of the State.

Section 6. Unreasonable Searches or Seizures. No authority shall be granted by the State to violate a person's right to privacy. Search and seizure of any property including cash, real estate, vehicles, personal items, memorabilia, paper documents, financial records, computers, phones or the content within shall be open to seizure only upon extreme proof of administration of justice to all, including the victim of seizure.

Section 7. Administration of Justice. No Court shall be secret. Justice shall be administered openly and without delay. Every person shall have availability of recourse and remedy for injustice imposed upon him by a court.

Section 8. Rights of the Accused in Criminal Prosecution. The accused shall have the right to the charge against him specified in writing. The accused shall have the right to face his accuser. The accused shall have the right to a jury trial in the county where said crime was committed. The decision of the jury in both verdict and sentencing shall not be overturned by the presiding judge.

Section 9. Double Jeopardy, Self-Incrimination. No person shall be tried twice for the same crime, or be compelled to testify against himself.

Section 10. Treatment of Arrested or Confined Person. No person arrested or confined in jail shall be physically, mentally or emotionally assaulted.

Section 11. Bail Bail will be available with sufficient surety for most offenses. Murder, assault or treason will be exceptions where the option of bail will not be available.

Section 12. Excessive Bail, Fines and Cruel and Unusual Punishment. Excessive bail and or excessive fines shall not be imposed. Cruel or unusual punishment shall not be inflicted. All penalties shall be proportionate to the offense, and shall fall within precedent. The court shall not instruct the jury at any time as to the law, or application of the law. It is in fact, the duty of the jury to evaluate both the law, and its application.

Section 13. Jury Trial in Civil Cases. In all civil cases, there is the right to a jury trial.

Section 14. Private Property Taken for Public Use. Property taken for public use will only occur after ample compensation has been negotiated and received by the owner.

Section 15. Services Taken for Public Use. No persons' service will ever be compelled for public use at any price.

Section 16. Imprisonment for Debt. No person shall ever be imprisoned for debt.

Section 17. Equality of Privileges and Immunities. No law shall be passed granting any citizen or class of citizens privileges, or immunities, that shall not be equal to all citizens.

Section 18. Laws Made After Contracts are Established (Ex-post Facto Laws). New laws made after contractual agreements are established, shall have no effect on those contracts.

Section 19. Suspension of Laws. Laws shall not be suspended by any authority, with the exception of the institution of Martial law. Habeas Corpus (The Ability to See the Incarcerated) shall never be suspended.

Section 20. Right to Assemble. Groups of any size may peaceably assemble for any purpose.

Section 21. Right to Bear Arms. All citizens shall have the right to bear arms for the defense of themselves, the State, and to keep the military in strict subordination to civil power.

Section 22. Immigration and Emigration. Immigration to the State can only be done by an American Citizen or Legal Immigrant to America. Anyone wishing to immigrate to the State must have proof of means of support so as to not become a burden on the State financially or medically. Medical or financial aid will not be provided under any circumstances to any person who has not established legal residence for a minimum of one year. Visitors needing emergency medical attention will receive such attention, but will be financially indebted to the State for such service. Immigrants must also pass an English literacy test since State provides no bilingual services. Emigration is always allowed. Once an Emigrant is gone for a period of one year, return is subject to same terms as any immigrant.

Section 23. Enumeration of Rights. Many rights are ethereal, such as "the right to feel emotion." Any such rights that may not be enumerated are not obstructed because of lack of enumeration.

Section 24. Slavery. A condition where the work or assets of one person are systematically and perpetually taken by another person or group with no acknowledgment and payment, as if by right, is illegal.

Section 25. Capital Punishment. When a defendant is unanimously found guilty, and the jury decides unanimously that capital punishment is the sentence, the defendant will have one year to appeal. The defendant will be allowed to request the service of any legal counsel in the United States for his/her defense. Upon agreement by that counselor to take the case, the State will provide funding to such counsel and its investigators. No license for such counselor is required. If the defendant is not exonerated within one year of sentencing, he/she will be executed at noon of that day.

Section 26. Sale of Liquor. Liquor can be sold by and from anyone to anyone over the age of 18.

Section 27. Activity for Prison Inmates The State shall not profit by labor from inmates.

For the purpose of human dignity and occupation of time, inmates are encouraged to participate in the infrastructure of the jail. Tasks such as laundry, cleaning, dining, library administration, exercise program administration, book club, religious services and other activities as may present themselves shall be offered to inmates to help minimize the banality of their prison incarceration, and create an environment for fostering normalcy for civil human interaction upon release. Businesses tend to hire former inmates who have shown a desire to work.

Educational opportunities may be offered by businesses. Businesses wishing to hire former inmates may wish to train such personnel during incarceration. This is encouraged. Businesses meeting the requirements to engage inmates for education may apply through the prison system, and inmates wishing to take advantage of these opportunities may apply for such programs. In our productivity based society, this is a win, win, win, situation for the inmate, the business, and the community.

Section 28. Parental Rights and Juvenile Crime. Parents are responsible for crimes committed by their children. The State does not wish to raise your child. Parents must take responsibility for their own children. If a parent wishes to give up a child for adoption, they may. A State school shall be instituted for such care and education of a child who has no parent or an irresponsible or criminal parent.

Parents wishing to raise their own children will take responsibility for that child's actions. Detailed statutes will be listed to describe the remedies for all crimes that may be committed by a person under the age of majority, eighteen. The goal of addressing this issue is to preserve the Parents' right to raise their own child. Rights carry responsibility. Children are a great responsibility. The State sincerely wishes for parents to retain this right, but will not allow the parent to deny the corresponding responsibility.

The State recognizes that the human nature of raising children is not instinctive. The State will institute highly flexible and dynamic programs designed for parents and children alike to make growing into adulthood happy, productive, emotionally satisfying, and as free of angst as is humanly possible. These programs will be at no cost to family members.

Section 29. Rights of Crime Victims The prosecution of criminals is highly adversarial by nature. Therefore, the rights of crime victims must be protected. The State recognizes that Families of the defendant or even gang members of the defendant may antagonize the victim. The victim must therefore be reasonably protected from any threats by such groups.

Defendants who are out on bail may be a threat to the victim. The Victim must also be notified and protected from defendants who are at large. Equally disturbing to the victim is the release of the perpetrator once that person is finished with jail time. The victim must be notified of prison release, and be reasonably protected from a perpetrator bent on revenge.

A victim protection program shall be instituted to protect people who have been victims of crime. Included in this protection process will be notification to the victim if the perpetrator dies. Even death of the perpetrator will not end the protection, as friends, gang, or family members may still carry a vendetta.

Section 30. Prison Term Exceptions Prisoners must serve the entire term of their sentence, but there are exceptions. The Governor may grant reprieves, commutations, clemency, or pardons. The Appellate Court may overturn the original ruling, usually due to new evidence.

This section does not provide remedies for harm or damage done to a person wrongfully convicted. The need for such remedy is recognized, but must be litigated in civil court. The recognition of wrongful conviction and incarceration, or even imposition of a fine, is not immediately recognized as a crime. If in the civil remedy process, crimes against the falsely convicted are discovered. The criminal prosecution process is then incorporated.

Section 31. Convicts as Jurors People formerly convicted of crimes cannot serve as jurors.

Article II (Why are we using Roman Numerals?)
Elections

Section 1. Elections are Free

Section 2. Qualifications Every Citizen 18 years of age or older, is qualified to vote in every election. The voter must present identification showing that he/she is a resident of the jurisdiction applicable to the specific election.

*****

As Ratzi Rige read down the literally 97 pages of the State Constitution he realized that there was a lot of stuff there that was needed to be specified, but in the Constitution?

Like Article XIV Section 1. If a guy terms out, in other words, his term is over, it's over. Even if the new guy can't take office because his election is contested, the old guy is still out. Now there's a gap, because he's out but nobody is in yet because of the contest. So in that case, another guy is temporarily appointed. Really! They thought of that. They actually voted and codified that. That's your tax dollars at work. Jesus, how many times is that going to happen? I mean really? Just have a vacancy for a while. Sheesh.

One thing that caught his eye was Article XI Section 1. Prohibition of State Banks.

The Legislative Assembly shall not have the power to establish, or incorporate any bank or banking company, or monied [sic] institution what so ever; nor shall any bank company, or instition [sic] exist in the State, with privilege of making, issuing, or putting in circulation, any bill, check, certificate, promisory [sic] note, or other paper, or the paper of any bank company, or person, to circulate as money.

First, wow, three typos in one section, those legislators should be ashamed of themselves, but more importantly, Ryan Chang was right.
We're not the Legislature
We're not a bank
And we're not printing paper and circulating it as money.
Our company club membership shopping exchange accounting system is Legal.

Just wait until we do fuel. The State tax on gasoline is thirty six cents a gallon and the tax on home heating oil is twenty four cents. I'm gonna buy a tanker full from Mexico and share it with my employees. They're gonna love the savings. Twenty gallon fill-up and you save $7.20. Damn.

Hundred gallons at home and you save $24.00. Yeah, people are gonna like that.

Note to self: Next time we call Amerada Hess to buy diesel for the ships, surreptitiously negotiate a deal on gasoline and home heating oil.

Here's another one, Article XV Section 5 Property of Women not subject to debts of husband. The property and pecuniary rights of every married woman, at the time of marriage or after-words, acquired by gift, devise, or inheritance shall not be subject to the debts, or contracts of the husband; and laws shall be passed providing for the registration of the wife's seperate [sic] property.

Another typo, where did these monkeys go to school? I mean, it's the Constitution.

Damn FemiNazis! They pull this gender biased stuff all the time. I wonder who were the *Manginas* were who voted this through. This section is in direct conflict with the Bill of Rights which states:

Article 1. Section 17. Equality of Privileges and Immunities. No law shall be passed granting any citizen or class of citizens' privileges, or immunities that shall not be equal to all citizens.

Orazio noticed his computer was acting up. He figured he had done enough for the day, and set the project aside.

Chapter Seven

Buy Your Votes

The battle for the best way to vote raged on across America. The Electoral College versus popular vote was a big issue. If you really wanted popular vote; if you really wanted Democracy, you would have each electoral vote counted separately, not lumped in with a state majority. The current system negates regional votes within states, especially the big ones.

California had its Top Two system which eliminated the Political Parties at the primary election level. In November, you would have only two choices, and your choice for State government officials might be both from the same Party. Most of the rest of America was unaware that a system like this was in place, and that the insanity of it was being promoted in the rest of the States. "As goes California, so eventually goes the rest of the country." It's a famous cliché. The idea of vote by mail, or, vote by computer was just one more way to encourage voter and election fraud. It was bad.

Orazio Rige had his own idea. It was revolutionary and would never ever be allowed by politicians, so Rige knew that all he had to do to try it was just change the world. No problem. He knew that the idea was so unique that it would take years of people talking about it before it would find support. He started with an op-ed.

Dear Friends and Neighbors, the reason there is no accountability from our legislators is because we have no contract with them. The reason that we don't have that contract is because we don't demand one.

The reason that money controls legislation is because we allow money to be given to legislators. Even if every legislator is not corrupt, the majority that is, easily runs over them. After a while, their noble efforts become pointless. They succumb to tolerance of this perversion because they don't want to lose their over-paid job.

What I propose is this:

Anyone can be a candidate. Registration is one dollar.

Ten issues are listed. Realize that some issues never go away. We had illegal immigration for decades. It was never addressed effectively because of no accountability. Believe me, if we can resolve even one issue it will be almost miraculous, so we set our goals at ten, and pray that at least one is achieved.

The ten issues will be decided by simple public polling. Politicians have been so ineffective in my lifetime that I am not concerned with corruption by the pollsters. The top few will be real at very least, and resolution of even one issue over each two year term will be an improvement over our current "do nothing" system. The top issue will be recognized and rise to priority by voter demand. If two issues are resolved, well, so much the better. Good luck to us all.

For 60 days, everyone can ask any question they want about those issues to all of the candidates.

Each candidate has 48 hours to respond to that question in Writing. If you can't do it in 48 hours, you are not leader material. You're out. The answer may be explained, but must be prefaced with a statement of positive or negative position. No ambiguity.

Each candidate's response is considered to be a legal contract with his voters.

Voting contrary to that contract, once in office, becomes cause for immediate dismissal from office, and the vote or proposed legislation becomes void.

Once the 60 days is over, voters have 60 days to "buy their votes."

There is a fortune of money spent on every election. Instead of spending it on media designed to fool, confuse or manipulate voters. The money will be given directly to the State, as stakeholders simply "Buy their Votes." Each vote will be ten dollars.

All the positions are known by the voters because of the sixty day interrogation and commitment period. It is pointless to campaign. Instead of committing vast sums of money to influence ignorant voters, you simply buy votes. Big money still wins, just as it does now, but instead of media getting the money, it goes to pay for medical care, education and infrastructure.

What will combat special interest money, will be unions of independent voters. The people will be compelled at last to become relevant. If the union of voters becomes strong enough, it will bankrupt the special interest. Special interests seeing this outcome will withdraw early or be ruined.

See how it works?

All money donated to political efforts will have immediate and equal value. Zero waste.

Since anyone can buy votes, there can be no voter fraud. People out of State or out of the country cannot buy votes. This is a cash windfall for the State, because all money from vote purchase goes to the State, not candidates grafting, or political Party slush funds.

Anyone making a vote purchase of over one thousand dollars will have to supply a written statement of the source of those funds, and be subject to possible investigation. Large purchases are welcome, but they will be known publicly and be scrutinized.

Out of State or out of Country money will be discovered. If somehow a clever person is able to supply money, at worst, that money will be in State coffers and not some person's. It may corrupt the election in that two year period, but will go a long way to providing money for the State so taxes can be lowered. The issue can come up again two years later, and either be defeated, or that clever donor will be continuing to fund the State's financial needs, lessening the burden on the people of the State until he is broke.

The vote tally is done and reported each day so there can be very little opportunity for election fraud.

There is no election day. At the end of the 60 days, the winners are simply known.

The tote board is a row of contestants, under which is a column of issues and responses. Once the first 60 days is over, the responses cannot be changed. The contestant can only resign. If the contestant resigns during the vote buying process, the vote money is returned to the vote buyer.

Since this streamlined system of addressing legislative duties will result in the elimination of many political positions, the size of government at this level will be drastically reduced. This will also result in massive tax savings for our production, as opposed to our consumption, based economy.

- Honesty in Campaigning
- Effective Legislative Body
- Reduced Cost
- Lower Taxes

It's a win win win win proposal for us.

The process is simply this:

First 30 day period, Issue Polls are taken

Next 60 day period, candidates make their contracts on the ten issues

Second 60 day period, votes are bought with full disclosure as to who has bought them, so that all can see who is exerting influence, and how serious the issues are being regarded.

(The State receives a massive influx of money, allowing roll back of taxes.)

The bought and paid for legislators take office.

They begin the process of resolving the ten issues. For every issue resolved, they each get $40,000 upon passage of law, based on their contract commitment to us.

If they resolve them all, they will receive $400,000 in their two year term. If they do nothing, they get nothing. There will be no other benefits. $200,000 per year is good money for the honor of public service, especially if they resolve the ten issues in ten weeks. They would effectively get the rest of the two years off with pay and our thanks. I'm sure millions of people would be happy to have such a job. Cooperation should be impressive. And we will get our money's worth.

Chapter Eight

Cyber Security

7:30 AM, Orazio Rige gets a phone call from Deanna Segal.

Deanna: Mr. Rige, there are three armed men in your inner office.

Orazio: Are you okay?

Deanna: Actually, I'm fine, not threatened, and in fact, I'm intrigued. They were here when I got here. They have only been here for ten minutes. They walked right through security and waited.

Orazio: Has security been called?

Deanna: Actually, they say that they are security. But Mr. Rige, I've never seen these guys before. They're totally calm. I'm under no duress and they brought coffee and food. They even brought some for us. They have already told me that you are on your way. They just wanted me to give you a heads-up, as crazy as it sounds, out of courtesy.

One of the men: Tell him not to break any speed laws getting here. We need the fifteen minutes anyway for something that just came up.

Orazio: They're right, I am about fifteen minutes out. Are you sure you're okay?

One of the men: Deanna please put me on speaker. I Orazio, I apologize for our behavior here, these other two wanted to show off. I know we're being rude, but our method has an inherent flair for the dramatic. Just get here, our meeting won't take too long, and I'm sure you'll be glad to meet me, and as for the other two, they're good guys. Oh, and we told Deanna we cancelled your first meeting this morning to make this time open for you. She'll contact the BSNF guys and reschedule. They were okay with the postponement. In fact, we're sure they're eager to work with you. You'll find out why, and we're going to give you an interesting leverage point that you can keep for your negotiations.

Fifteen minutes later, Orazio strode into the room to find three skinny guys with coffee, pastries, breakfast sandwiches on the table, and Deanna laughing her head off.

Orazio: Wow, I didn't expect everyone to be laughing.

Deanna: This gentleman has told us more than a half a dozen jokes in the last five minutes.

Orazio: Well buddy, it's a hell of an ice-breaker huh? How about you give me the bottom line and we can work backwards from there.

One of the men: First, you are not in any danger from us.

Orazio: So, why are you visibly armed?

One of the men: Right. That's not for you. That's for the people watching us. The arms are just a defensive prop. We're constantly at risk so we stand ready. Mr. Joke Meister over there is actually a very good strategist when it comes to getting out of trouble. The guy who is not joking is listening. His job is to make sure no one else is. And congratulations, this office was secure. But first, as you suggested, let me give you the reason for our visit and then you can have a thorough Q and A.

What's happening right now is there is a tanker ship coming to you full of Mexican fuel. That ship has been diverted to a harbor in San Francisco by a group who call themselves The Axis. The Axis is our nemesis, or we're there's depending on which side you're on. Your cargo is being stolen by them on behalf of a powerful political organized crime family group there. It's complicated, but you'll get it. The politicians don't want you or your money. That's not why this is happening. They simply don't want you to rise to power. They're nipping you in the bud as it were. This is just a demonstration of resolve by them. Hell, if you're contrite, they may even give you back your oil.

Orazio: What do you mean being diverted? Should we call the Coast Guard? And who are you in this picture?

One of the men: You can call us The Ten. Coast Guard, if it were only that easy. The San Francisco Family hires The Axis because they are really detailed perpetrators of crime in plain sight. If the Coast Guard were to inspect the ship, it's orders and manifest, it would find everything in perfect order. All the paperwork involved in this from beginning to end has been redone by The Axis. To anyone coming into the picture at this point, the ship is doing exactly what you ordered. You're going to find that you are even going to be charged the docking, offload and transportation costs incurred in your deal. That's how bad this is going to be. You're going to hear about it through your channels later today.

Orazio: This is all just too farfetched. I don't know you. I've never heard of anything like this. I…...

The Ten interrupt: We know. Take a deep breath. This is a lot to take in.

Orazio: I can't believe that you told me all this in front of my secretary.

The Ten: Oh, Deanna? She's totally trustworthy, and we're saving you the trouble of explaining all this to her. We would have asked Donna and Marla Black to join us, but they're in D.C. and we kinda do everything in person. You understand. Eluding The Axis is not easy, but we have it down to a science, at least until they change the science.

Oh, and by the way, those Black sisters are really good at what we both do, but they do it in hard copy as opposed to with computers. It's totally caveman, but they are gifted in a kinda lost-art way. Their ability to hide their tracks and make discrete off-the-record deals is amazing. They do their stuff real cloak and dagger. It's like watching a James Bond movie or Mission Impossible; the real one, not the Tom Cruise ones. We love 'em.

Orazio: So who's this crime family?

The Ten: Do we have to tell you? They operate in plain sight. We all let them. We elect them. We have for years.

Orazio: Okay, and who's The Axis?

The Ten: They call themselves Mauser and Yukawa, after a German gun and a Japanese physicist. Germany and Japan were once called the Axis powers. Childish right? Obviously avatars. We believe they are from India because of the British English they sometime let slip, and some of the Hindu religious references they have made.

These guys are real. They work out of a submarine. How many regular people do you know who can man a submarine, or even get one? The sub is an Indian Navy Arihant Class

66

prototype. It has no armaments. It was supposedly destroyed. Apparently not. The sub usually has a crew of well over a hundred men, but being that most of the sub's resources are not used, their crew is probably more like twenty.

These guys are dangerous sociopaths. They are unpredictable and their motivations are always impossible to guess. They are a weird combination of gun-for-hire and video game enthusiast. We believe from personality profile work we have done that they have a complete detachment from reality and humanity. And when I say complete detachment, that characterization is not to be taken lightly. They are truly playing a different game than anything you can imagine. The reasoning of a sociopath can never be predicted by the rational thinking person. All we can do is anticipate any possibility and create a response to it. Sometime we guess right, and sometime we don't.

We've already protected the Black sisters a few times, but it's time they come to know what's up. Don't worry, we'll tell them. In fact, we might be telling them right now.

Orazio: So The Ten is more than just you? Is it seven more?

The Ten: The Ten is not a body count. It's just a name.

Orazio: Are you government?

The three men of The Ten all laugh, then say: No. We move too quickly for bureaucracy. We're our own agency. We're cut from the same cloth as The Axis in that we're all computer Geeks. For us, this is a game too. The difference is very much a question of where is your reality. If you think that the virtual world is real, you are The Axis. I don't know where they think their food comes from, but apparently, they don't care. They just take. We know that we need farmers or we starve, so we protect them. We protect all infrastructures, because The Axis is not the only group capable of worldwide anarchy through computer tampering. Someone has to fight outside government because people like The Axis are.

Orazio: So you're some high-tech altruists?

The Ten: No, we're a for profit business just like you.

Orazio: How are you funded?

The Ten: Money? That's easy. A few of us are really good at cleaning up financial carrion. A guy dies with no heirs. The government is eventually going to clean out his accounts. We do it first. Businesses die and have outstanding accounts or receivables. We get 'em. We bring closure, and in the process, we tie up loose ends that just fill the world with a weird junkyard of inconsequential past. Very few people ever see the results of our cleanups, and those who do, are always bottom-feeding lawyers or accountants who many times have made the messes to begin with, and want to profit by them. We love screwing those types. It's the equivalency of poetry in our world. Do you ever wonder who eats dead vultures?

Orazio: I wonder why two guys from India called themselves The Axis.

The Ten: Trying to find reason in the behavior of the sociopath? You lose. You can't help what you just did. It's normal. You have to get used to thinking abnormally, without being infected yourself. I know you understand this, but it is hard to work with. Don't worry, that's what we're here for. We have the virtual-antibodies to the virtual virus.

Orazio: What the …, if what you're saying is true, what do we do about my oil? How do I know it's not you stealing the oil? You could be the sociopathic thief flaunting …..

The Ten interrupt: Right! Bingo! Now you're getting it. See how hard it is to play. You're entering the disinformation trap. Say we say, look Ratzi, do nothing about the oil, we'll figure it out. Hell, you can't trust us. That would be insane …..

Another member of The Ten interrupts: Excuse me, the ship has changed course. It's routed to Frisco now.

The Ten: Look, Mr. Rige. You will be notified by your own people momentarily. Do exactly what you think is best. You have to. The Axis, hopefully, doesn't know that we are here. So be normal. Fight, just as you're supposed to. The Axis doesn't need to be tipped off that we're on to them. Take care of yourself as best you can. This meeting is over. We'll be in touch.

They got up, each making eye contact, nodding, bowed slightly to Deanna Segal, and moved out.

Orazio Rige immediately turned on the security monitor camera screens on his wall to watch then leave. Every screen showed none of them, like they were never there.

He and Deanna looked out the window to see them enter an arriving car. He couldn't identify the model, but there was something about the driver that looked familiar.

Chapter Nine

Factory Tour

The call did come. Orazio and Deanna sat there and listened while the ship captain asked him what the hell he was doing. Orazio told him "full stop' right where you are. Right there in the water, stop. Do not pull that ship into the harbor.

The captain told him, it's not that easy. We have contracts with the crew. They're not just going to sit here without an explanation. They have commitments that require them to get off the ship. Some of them will be happy if they don't have another gig. For them it's easy money, but for the others, they're going to have issues.

Orazio told the captain not to worry, and that he would make good as always. The captain knew it was true. Orazio told Deanna to call the managers in charge of the project. In the meantime, he had a question that was more on his mind. He called Oscar Rodriguez.

Orazio: Hi Oscar.

Oscar: Hey Boss, I figured you'd be calling me. Did you see my limo?

Orazio: Your limo?

Oscar: Did you see the car my boys came and went in?

Orazio: Your car? Your Boys? Yeah, I just saw a car I didn't recognize. That's what I'm calling about. How are those guys, your boys?

Oscar: Did you get a good look at the car? That's your car man. That's the Toad limo. We stretched one. When Bobby asked for a ride for his friends, we hooked him up with that car.

Orazio: Who is Bobby?

Oscar: Bobby Diez man. He's my kids' computer science teacher. We're so tight with him that he asked us to see if you would hire his friends. He told us that three of them had an appointment with you. He asked us to hook them up with a ride. So what do you think of the car?

Orazio: Okay look, I'm way too far out of the loop on this. Why don't you tell me the story of who everybody is and how you know them.

Oscar: Oh shit, was there a problem?

Orazio: No, uh, I just wish I knew to look at the car. I didn't go down after the meeting. I just saw it from the window, and they were already here when I got here.

Oscar: Yeah, we put the car in the parking structure and covered it because we didn't want too many people to see it yet. I'm sorry. Hey, we're making one for Carole Koz; a little one for her. Around here we call it the tadpole. It's almost ready. She's gonna turn heads man.

Orazio: Oscar, who is Bobby?

Oscar: Bobby Diez? Here's what happened. Our band was playing and this guy came up to us and asked if he could come to our place one day and jam a taste. We like that, so we said sure. The guy had computers. He was a keyboard guy, but not like a piano player. I mean this guy had an orchestra in his laptop. He made us sound like the L.A. Phil, you know what I mean? He was baller dude. He was a real computer freak. We don't really need that because we rock out old school, but he was making a lot of music on a crazy techno level.

Our kids saw him, and they were trippin. They never saw anything like him. We have kids in school in Bend you know? So in their school, they have a computer science class, but it's kinda slow going because not all the kids learn at the same rate. Some of our kids are crazy sharp with that shit, and we all live right next door to each other, so Bobby asked if we would let him home-school all our kids, you know, just on the computer stuff. They still go to regular school for everything else. We thought it might be great and it was. Our kids are like computer geniuses. They make their own games and write their own programs. They use the computer code. It's actually like another language. They're the balls with it. So Bobby asked me if his friends could come see you. They told us they had an appointment, and they knew all about the Toad, because when we launch the cars for real, our kids are gonna make the whole world know on day one.

Orazio knew he had to play it cool.

Orazio: That's an incredible story Oscar, congratulations on everything. I've been ignoring you for far too long. You guys aren't getting my attention because you don't create any problems. That's backward right? I feel bad. I'll tell you what. I'm gonna come out there right now.

Orazio covered the phone and said to Deanna, "Get Koz."

I want you to bring me up to date on everything. You got time for me?

Oscar: For Mr. Rige, anything. Wait 'til you see what's here. We're spending your money good.

72

Orazio: Okay, give me a few hours.

Oscar: Hey, take your time, and if you want to stay over, you should. We got a lot going on. We want to show you our plans. We're gonna need a lot more money. We're gonna hit you up.

Orazio: I feel like everybody is setting me up today.

Oscar: Only the smart ones right? Hey rich boy, it comes with the job. You wouldn't want it any other way would you?

Orazio: Oscar, I love ya. You're gonna give me good news aren't you?

Oscar: Always. See ya later.

And Oscar hung up.

Orazio said to Deanna, "He ended the call."

Deanna: Well, *mucho macho.*

Orazio: The guy's a brilliant engineer with no credentials and bad grammar.

Deanna: Brains and drive got nothing to do with money. That Homie ain't nobody's fool.

Orazio just looked long at her, and said, "*Diez* means ten doesn't it?"

Carole Kozlowski walked into the office.

Carole: Hey handsome, feeling lonely?

73

Orazio: You always know what to say. Yeah, lonely. I hear you're getting a new car.

Carole: That was supposed to be a surprise. Oscar said to me, "I know the boss wants to take care of his lady first. He's all American, but he's an Italian a heart." I told him, "I'm not his lady," and he said, "Bitch, please."

He asked me what kind of car the boss wants to see me in. I asked him if he knew who Emma Peel was. He said, "Oh, you want a Lotus Elan?" I said back, "No, you asked me what Ratzi wants." And Oscar said, "Oh, and you're gonna give him what he wants?" That Oscar is a real little smart-ass isn't he?

Orazio: He's completely unafraid of either one of us.

Carole: That's what makes him one of us. It's important that you remember that.

Being one of us is easier than being one of them. He's gonna come through for you with a loyalty you can't buy. It's his test of your manhood. You have to match him, or you ain't shit. He came here with nothing but respect for himself and love of his extended family. He maintains that, and has given you unearned respect but the test is on. He's giving you a chance to earn his respect, and the respect of his family. If you stand up right at every turn, you'll be part of a family. It's heavy. There are a lot of them Orazio, and they all understand this. *Entiende usted?*

Orazio: Do I understand? Probably not like you. Are they testing you?

Carole: The men are building me a car Ratzi. I'm gonna wear it like an engagement ring. The women? You don't want to know that test. Have you heard the expression "Blood in blood out?"

Orazio: I've heard it.

Carole: They live it.

Orazio: We're heading there right now.

Carole: Not dressed like this we're not. Your suit is okay, but I need comfortable clothes. We are staying overnight. They're gone to offer and we're going to accept. You're going to sleep in the shop, and I'm going to stay with *tia Maria*.

Orazio: Actually, I have a crisis with a ship that has to be taken care of, I can't stay. Plus, I have to have a serious meeting with the Blacks.

Carole: Well, they'll be disappointed but understand. You can go back. They'll give me a ride or a car, God knows they have plenty of 'em. But Ratzi, you seem very upset. What's up?

Orazio: I got thrown a few curve balls, and I'm momentarily not in control. Do I need to take you back home to grab some stuff?

Carole: No, I always have an overnight bag in my office closet, you know, in case of an apocalypse.

Orazio: Deanna …

Deanna interrupted, "I got it. Go."

Orazio took a box of pastries and a bottle of water left by The Ten, walked Carole to her office, and then to his Lincoln.

*****

The ride out to Prineville was relaxing. Orazio told Carole Koz all about The Ten, and the surprise visit. He told her what he was being told, and that Donna and Marla Black were being told. Told exactly what, he was not sure. He knew he was going to run into trouble, but never imagined this clandestine information organization and that the organization would be in competition with another such organization, somehow hired by corrupt politicians .... it just seemed far-fetched, for a straight-shooter businessman like him.

Carole introduced the fact that he dabbled in politics. He dabbled in changing their power structure. She reminded him that at the top level, politics served industry, and symbiotically, industry supported politicians. It's a game of manipulation. A politician, the media, the regular people, or in other words the voters, and industry, all play, who's got the leverage. Look at Dana Morea. She dances with all that doesn't she?

Orazio realized that he was just handed a whole new set of players whom he did not know. His rompin' stompin' legal team seemed very small all of a sudden. Even his wealth seemed to no longer be the thing that would allow him to call the shots. It was like a mysterious stranger you meet who is intriguing but dangerous. At this point he had only computer dated his strangers. Now, the computer itself was the date.

Orazio thought on it. He asked Carole, did you ever date a computer? She said no. He said, "I did." She asked him to tell her about that. He asked, "Do you know chess Carole?" Carole told him she knew how to play the game and asked why. He asked her if she had ever played chess with a computer. She told him no. Then he said, "The way it works is this. Someone puts full games into the computer. Very many chess games are the same game played over and over. When the computer recognizes which historic game you are playing, it knows what to do to win. The trick is, to do something unexpected. Now the computer must think. But the computer cannot think, but it must continue, because the game is not over. It makes a move hoping that your next move will put the board once again in a position where it can recognize the game and thereby win. It's got an incredible memory, but you are unpredictable and must remain so. Given enough time, the computer will figure out moves that lead to victory. But if there is a time limit, you can win. We have to be unpredictable here. We always follow the law. That is our weakness. Today, that's over."

Carole said, "I think you are going to meet the right people today. I think they are going to help you a lot." She had a smile that Orazio knew well. Carole was holding some winning cards. She said, "Let me call Oscar and tell him we are almost here."

When the Lincoln pulled up at the front of the car facility, they were there standing at attention like a military reception. Oscar introduced them. Mateo, Santiago, Matias, Angel, Benjamin, Martin, Nicolas, Alejandro, Lucas, Diego, and Leonardo, the original twelve. This was Toad. He asked Orazio to stand in the middle, six on each side for a picture. He said, "*Jefe*, today we're making you an honorary Mexican. At least your name ends in a vowel. *Felicidades.*" Oscar took out a bottle of Tequila, poured a shot into 13 plastic cups. Everybody raised theirs, and took a quick swallow.

By this time, Carole was surrounded by women and she was off to who knows where.

The guys all went into the car factory and stood there with all the pride in the world. First, the place was immaculate. Next, finished cars were in what could only be the showroom. The rest of the layout was self-explanatory;

Mateo's frame shop,
Santiago's suspension shop,
Matias's motor shop,
Angel's drive train shop
Benjamin's wheel and brake shop
Martin's cowl shop
Nicolas's sheet metal and glass shop
Alejandro's body assembly shop
Lucas's upholstery shop
Diego's wiring shop
Leonardo's paint and finish shop
And Oscar's office.

The place was beehive busy with technicians. Each station had a half a dozen guys working. How could this be? Oscar was looking at Orazio and just waiting.

Orazio said to Oscar, "Oscar, who is paying all these men?" Oscar said back, "Mr Rige, you don't know the half of it." He then asked Orazio to step into a small electric golf cart, and Oscar took him through the factory slowly, and out in the back. The factory was 1,000 feet wide by 250 feet deep. From the road, it hid a lot on the gently down sloping back grade. Behind the 250,000 square foot factory and a thousand feet down the hill was another beehive of activity, this time, home construction. Another hundred or so men were building houses.

Orazio said to Oscar, "Mr. Rodriguez, let me have it."

Oscar: Well Mr. Rige, this is what happened. We needed more guys almost right away, so we began to ask our cousins and friends to come up here from L.A. Well, word got around, so people began to actually ask us if we had a place for them. By the way, we need more room in the factory. We can mass produce these cars no problem, probably one or two a day just with hand tools. Figure five hundred a year as soon as you're ready at twenty thousand per car. That's ten million dollars just with what we have now.

Oscar continued to drive the golf cart down the incline.

We made the first car in a month and used all the batteries that my brother had. The batteries worked perfect, so we knew we had a good thing. We had a few friends who were out of work anyway, so we brought them up here and they worked for beer. We didn't care. We made a little money here and there with our car business that we do anyway. It was okay. Then the Blacks bought all this land down here on spec. It was dead land but they knew you would give them the right of way, so it would be opened up. They also had the variance for the pipeline to the ocean so we knew water was coming. Dana Morea had something figured with the water table that would make her lake drain into wells here from underground. We had to wait for the water, but you know, waiting is hard, so we got some of our guys to help the company that was building the pipeline. It was all cool. We got that done about three months ago.

Well, you already know about Bobby Diez. He came along and said that if we built him a house back here, he would buy all the materials to build one each for the twelve of us, and The Black sisters donated the land. All we needed was the labor. We went back to L.A. and found all these home construction guys who were fucked over by divorce court. Look at the job they're doing. It's all barter.

Orazio: Oscar, there are building codes and permits.

Oscar: Oh, the Blacks have all that stuff sewed up. We're in business and so are you. When you want to market the cars, our kids will sell them right away online. In fact, because it's limited production we're probably going to have bidding that will start at $20,000 and go up. We have the batteries, and Marla has all the legal protection. Donna has the intellectual property patents for the countries that have the capability to make knock offs, so we're pretty sure that we can go kinda right now.

One of the things that we want to hit you up for is the factory for the batteries, because that's the real business. That's the zillion dollar deal. The car is just the window dressing. I mean, I know you know all this but I'm just summarizing for my own sake. I'm really just the car guy. You guys can revolutionize the energy industry. I just want the batteries. It all came fast Mr. Rige, mostly because we were able to get all this cheap, off the books, skilled labor. Those pipe guys made the whole power plant thing happen like magic. Some of them were former convicts who couldn't get work and were happy to just get out of a bad scene in town. We shook a little at first, but nobody gave us no trouble, because everybody just worked together, and they still are. I mean, we got a crew here.

Orazio: What are you going to do for sewer lines?

Oscar: Oh, Rods girlfriend Dana has that all worked out. That was the first thing we did before pouring any of this foundation concrete. This whole grid is piped for drainage.

Orazio: Streets?

Oscar: Someday. Right now, it doesn't rain here much so we're okay on dirt roads. You know, one of the things I like about these construction guys is, they live in these Winnebago's. They don't even need to commute. They park right in front of the place they're working on. We have a place out in back of the shop where they can service their vehicles with water and sewage, and guess what, they all have the helium batteries, yeah right. These guys run air conditioning and electric heat for a month without a charge, and with the geo power, the charge is free. See that house right there, the closest one to the shop?

Orazio: Yeah.

Oscar: That one is mine. It's almost ready. Xiomara can't believe it.

Chapter Ten

Aliens on Board

Meanwhile, in the calm Pacific Ocean just west of San Francisco, the DEA was approaching the Mexican tanker ship. Two armed ships were coming up alongside, one to port, one to starboard. The starboard vessel called the captain of the tanker, and instructed him to assemble his crew on that side of the ship and prepare to be boarded. The ship's deck guns were not trained on the tanker for safety reasons, but the men coming on board were heavily armed with heavy caliber automatic rifles and wore combat body armor.

The crew assembled. "They're all accounted for," the DEA agent said, looking at his own list, and escorted the group to the dining room where they were held, and taken one by one to another room for interrogation. The captain asked why this was happening. The DEA Special Unit Officer I (One), and a Special Forces Captain, as recognized by their name tags, told the ship's captain to sit down and told him that he was not under arrest, but would be advised to be silent and comply as instructed until a thorough search of his ship was completed. He didn't seem to have any choice. He asked if he could contact his company. The Special Forces Captain told him he had ten seconds to yell into the wind as loud as he wanted and then he would have to shut up. With that, the Ship Captain knew something was very wrong.

The door to the cabin opened, and another DEA Officer instructed the ship's captain to come with him. They hustled down into the hold of the ship, and there they found thirty Mexicans all huddled together. The DEA Officer asked, "Do you want to explain this?" The Captain was taken completely off guard. The DEA officers were smiling at him. He knew he was being had. He said, "*Alqarf.*" (Shit)

All the illegal immigrants in the steel walled unventilated room were silent. One guy just looking at the floor said softly, "*Hal tatakalam alearabia. La tanzur 'iilaya.*" (You speak Arabic, don't look at me.) The Captain understood.

The ship Captain was isolated in his own room and left alone. After a few minutes he heard a tap, tap tap, tap tap tap on the door. He went to the door and said, "Arm the Mexican with the yellow and green bandana around his neck." He heard one of the DEA ships pull away and leave the scene. He wondered what his own combat brother, the man outside his door would do. He always kept his friend from the war in Damascus with him. They suffered from two traumas; one; combat, two; divorce court. Left in society with punk judges, the soldier would soon find logic in taking the battle to those judges on his terms, but maybe administering a little too much justice. He couldn't let that happen, so they stayed together. Their brotherhood was the only think that made sense to them. It was all the reality they could hold onto having been betrayed by their country by being separated from their own children.

The soldier managed to quietly and harmlessly replace one of the DEA agents with himself. The DEA men were so heavily hidden in their helmets and face masks that they couldn't identify each other. He walked right into the prisoners' hold room and said to the man with the yellow and green bandana. "You, come with me." He brought the man out into the hallway and handed him the knife and gun he had taken from the mercenary he had incapacitated. The man wasn't a Mexican. He was a Syrian. The Syrian told the Captain's brother in arms, "These men are not DEA." He got back an appreciative wink. By his count, there were sixteen mercenaries on the tanker, and the tanker was big. They would be spread out. None of them would guess there were two combatants. They had the element of surprise. Tactically, he would have to wait until the Syrian soldier made his move.

There was no time to make a plan, but he knew what the Syrian would do, enemy personnel attrition. Kill the killers before they kill you.

He didn't have to wait long. A general alert sounded and for the soldier, he knew the battle was on. Mission one; free the Captain. Mission two; protect the crew and Mexicans who could become hostages. He went down to the hold where the Mexicans were being kept. The door was not locked, but they were all still there. Fortunately for him, many of them spoke pretty good English. He explained quickly and got them to move to another room on the ship where they would be safe.

The room the regular ship's crew was in was tactically strong. Once the shooting started, they would barricade themselves in. Only gas could choke them out, and he was pretty sure the mercenaries weren't that ready. At least he took the risk. Next he went to his own hideout and contacted the Coast Guard. He told them the ship was under siege by fake DEA, and to proceed with extreme caution. A second pirate ship under false flag may appear and engage so heads up. Then he heard it, the barrage of gun fire. He knew the Syrian was pinned down. He didn't have time to rescue the Captain; he had a man in trouble.

Running toward the fight, he fired two different weapons to simulate a gunfire exchange. There were just too many of them to draw them all off. He knew the Arab was running out of ammo. He threw a box of explosives into the ocean with a live hand grenade in it. As it went off with multiple explosions, the mercenaries assumed the tanker was under attack from another ship. They abandoned the Arab to head back to their own ship. As they got to the side, ready to climb back to the escape ship, they found it had moved a few hundred feet away from the tanker. Somebody had cut it loose. The Captain had gotten free and had engaged the battle by doing this. The men on board the drifting ship were trying to get it back into position when the horizon showed a Coast Guard Heritage Class Offshore Patrol Cutter moving in fast. They were stuck. They didn't have time to rescue their crew and run, but didn't have the man power to fight the Coast Guard without them. They chose to rescue their crew, but they knew a fire fight would never work. They prayed they had the fuel to outrun the coming vessel, but as the saying goes, you can't outrun cannons.

Soon helicopters and other ships corralled the mercenary ship. The Coast Guard boarded the tanker. Everybody was on deck on their backs, hands behind their heads, and big smiles on their faces.

Coast Guard: Do you have any wounded?

Captain: No sir.

Coast Guard: You the Captain?

Captain: Yes sir.

Coast Guard: Is everyone accounted for?

Captain: Yes sir. 22 registered Crew, my personal bodyguard Jim, 29 South Americans seeking political refuge, 1 Syrian refugee who served our ship above and beyond the call of duty, sir. The pirates he killed were killed in self-defense. I will attest to that. It was not murder. He served as a soldier, our soldier.

Coast Guard: Do you see any reason why your complement and passengers need to be prostrate?

Captain: No, they just didn't want any misunderstandings as you came aboard, actually now, they're just resting.

The Coast Guard Officer addressed the men on deck. "Men you are now under the protection of the United States Coast Guard. Your worries are over. Please feel free to move, but stay here while we secure the ship."

Coast Guard: Do I need to repeat that in Spanish?

Captain: No, they have had enough trouble being hijacked and abused. They're not going to make trouble. They want to eat, get cleaned up, sleep, and make their case as to why we need them in our country.

Coast Guard: Can I trust your crew to make that personal care part happen?

Captain: Probably better than you.

Coast Guard: Captain, we have to inspect your ship.

Captain: You bet you do. I demand it. Who knows what booby traps or contraband they may have left? Be careful. We don't want any of you getting hurt.

Coast Guard: You served didn't you?

Captain: Yes sir, Damascus, the hub of the shithole. Check out the Syrian. Check him out good. If he passes muster, I'll sponsor him myself. If he doesn't check out, it will be with my great regret that you will have to do what you have to do.

And sir, when we're clear, we'd appreciate an escort to Coos Bay. The paperwork will say San Francisco, but that was part of the pirate trap. We just want to complete the original mission.

Coast Guard: Right! I'll take it under advisement.

Orazio got the news. So did Amerada Hess.

*****

Rige Coos Bay would never be the same. Orazio wanted to bring forth advancement for mankind. His intentions were truly altruistic. He was being fucked-with by people he just didn't understand. When I say he didn't understand, I'm not saying he was naïve. He knew that oil companies would never allow innovations that would put them out of business. He knew that politicians could never allow an outside entity to gain power without the proper tribute. He knew it, but it was a case of, until it happens to you .....

He was just a man of "better nature." He was a builder of prosperity, farms and factories, not defensive castles and fortresses. He had dealt with plenty of corrupt bureaucrats, but they were always so easy to just pay off or have his lawyers confound them. He never had to deal with guys with guns. It was always just civilized business, fair enough. Rige Coos Bay would never be the same. "You want to strike from the shadows and bring on physical attacks instead of legal attacks, I have Mafiosi for that," he thought. "You wanna get weird and dirty? I'll show you weird and dirty. He began to write a list of his friends. First among them was Matty. He realized that since he loved so many, he was vulnerable in as many ways. Strategically, his lifestyle made him tragically vulnerable. He had too much to protect, his friends, and all of them in the wide open.

He called Carole Kozlowski. He needed to think and as usual, he needed to think out loud. She walked into the office happy and beautiful. Orazio felt suddenly relaxed. It's wonderful how the familiar can make you feel. Sometime, just a song from the past can really remind you of who you are. Sometime, you can feel really good about yourself just from a reminiscent smell. Carole was all that. Bodyguards can make you feel safe from harm, but Carole made Orazio feel safe from self-doubt.

He said, "Carole, I need to take stock." She nodded, and he began.

We have our politicians taking control of the State from the backdoor. Am I deluding myself in thinking this is progress?

We have a big box store company that is growing using what is essentially our own currency. How big a threat is that to the national money system?

We have a geo-thermal electric plant running independently, producing electricity cheaper than anyone in the nation. Are we threatening anybody?

We are irrigating the desert at no cost. Does the State Water Department resent us?

We have a secret battery that is going to tip over the world soon. Who will be our biggest opponent? The Blacks have secured international patents around the world, but we all know that our "secret technology" will be reverse engineered and pirated immediately. How do we fight that?

We have a car company that will shock the world with economy, efficiency, and style. I'm so proud of the visionary idea those guys gave us that I don't even care if it booms or busts. I just love watching them work. They're out there building a city around their dream. It's commitment on a level of faith in them-selves that is the definition of American fortitude. Why are they building a car for you before building one for me? I'm happy for you. It's fun to be jealous sometime.

We have angry government criminals hijacking my cargo because they're not ready to put a horse's head in my bed. How do I address that?

We have two weird computer hacking sociopathic geek gamers playing with our real life. One of them employed mercenary pirates on behalf of a San Francisco politician crime family to get the attention of the other computer gamers who say they are working on our side? Who do we have who we can trust who can begin to get me in that game?

"Stop right there," Carole said. "Donna and Marla are going to introduce you to your new girlfriend as soon as they get back in town. This woman runs an international prostitution ring that has worked with them to undermine the power of all kinds of international players. The woman needs protection. We're going to park her at your house for the ensuing siege. The reason I tell you this at this moment is because the Blacks have worked with The Ten and have all the dirt they need to shut down the creeps in San Fran. The strategy is underway. It will take time, but will keep those maggots busy. They are very powerful and should not be underestimated. You know the cliché, when you wrestle a pig in the mud, you both get dirty, but the pig loves it. The Ten know about the battery. They respect it's yours. Anyway, manufacturing is not their game."

Orazio: How come you know more about what's going on than I?

Carole: Because I'm not running a company, I have time to keep tabs on your interests. Everybody is doing their job. It's all happening quickly, and it has too. The battery is the real world changer. Everything is ancillary to that.

Orazio: I guess we have a full plate and there is no more reason for you to headhunt?

Carole: Are you kidding? I have two more STEM kids waiting for your time. The two best yet.

Orazio: Really? How can anything beat the helium battery?

Carole: Both do.

Chapter Eleven

Lana

Out at the geo-thermal plant in Prineville, ocean water that was pumped with tidal pressure pumps from the Pacific Ocean was being used to cool the turbines of the electric generators. The pumps were so efficient that a salt water lake was slowly being filled in a natural deep valley. The water that was boiled to cool the pumps was creating a natural distillation process as steam was deposing its salt content in a hopper as it escaped through the cooling piping. Water coming out of the steam pipes was salt free, and was piped out to another valley where it was being used to irrigate a field a few miles away. Dana Morea was irrigating a planned forest. Pine trees were being planted in a pattern as the fresh water was softening the land.

To transform a desert to a forest, the land has to be able to hold water. In a pine forest, the falling needles cover the ground and eventually nothing else can grow. It's how pine trees naturally capture all the water for themselves and hold it. Dana covered the area between the trees with a ground covering plant that didn't use much water. She knew that one day the trees would kill those plants, but also knew that they would make a wonderful peat under the needle bed that would nourish the trees for years. All they needed was a little irrigation to get the cycle of microbial life rolling. Dana had that water, and once the trees were established, just a few hundred yards of iron pipe added in different directions would allow the forest to expand. The beautiful Morea Pine Woods was to be her legacy gift to Mother Earth.

*****

Carole took Orazio out to Bend Municipal Airport to meet his new girlfriend?
What?

Lana, as she was to be called, was a very dear friend of Marla and Donna Black. She ran a very upscale escort service all around the world and was originally employed by the Blacks to help influence the various patent agents whose cooperation had been needed for expedient clerical work regarding their little battery thingy. It seemed to be a win-win for everybody until some trouble started that got out of hand, making the lady a marked woman.

The Ten had created a completely new identity for Lana. Even though she was of Polish ancestry on her mother's side, she spoke fluent Russian, you know, for business, so they called her Svetlana Pavlichenko. She was to have met Orazio through a "Russian Matrimonial" computer dating service. It was all quite believable. She was beautiful, and Orazio's age, if her fake age was to be believed. They were a sharp couple. She needed a place to hide out and with Orazio; she could hide in plain sight.

As the Cessna Citation CJ3 was landing, Carole told Orazio that Lana was not up for grabs. The relationship was to be completely professional. Lana was not interested in romance so even though there may be plenty of that in public, there wouldn't be any in the house. Carole said that she knew Orazio would be relieved to hear that, RIGHT RATZI?

Orazio said, "Oh yeah, the last thing I would want is any kind of romantic relationship with a professional lover." And Carole said back, "I knew you would feel that way." Both of them blushed. Not outwardly. They both just got that warm inside feeling when you know you are caught doing something nice for each other that can't be expressed with humble dignity. We don't really have a word in English for a moment like that, do we? Such expressions made them more in love than ever.

Lana stepped out of the airplane onto the stairs and looked as powerful as Jackie Kennedy coming out of Air Force One. She waved using the "Miss America Wave." Orazio thought he had never seen Carole roll her eyes before. He liked it. He liked it a lot. Lana was striking. Orazio asked, "Wouldn't it have been smarter to be a little more low key Carole?" Carole said back, "She didn't look like this when she got on the plane. She took a commercial flight to Houston. We slipped her onto this plane there with her single suitcase. Her considerable luggage will be arriving separately. The Ten orchestrated the whole thing. That's the good news and the bad news. I still don't know what to make of those guys. They come through for us too well. To them, it's a game. The attitude is not comforting. Usually I can read anybody. These guys? I can't get them off balance; can't get 'em to show their cards. Their motivations are just unknown."

Both Carole and Orazio greeted Lana with a warm hug. Carole opened the back door of the Lincoln for her. Orazio opened the front passenger door for Carole and tried to take Lana's case to put it in the trunk. Lana wouldn't let go, shook her head no, and Orazio let her keep it with an affirming nod. Lana said, "Orazio it's nice to meet you and so nice of you to have come to get me in person. I really just expected a car." Orazio leaned back and over his shoulder said, "Expected? I don't know what to expect anymore. That's part of the problem. When we get home, I expect you to tell me, or us if Carole is going to stay, a lot of stories. As you know, we have a lot going on. My people are all so good that they can operate without me supervising their every move, but now, we have people working for us that we don't even know. I'd like to think I can rein that in, but frankly, I'm not sure who's in charge. Everything we're doing, we're doing for the right reason, and until now, I've felt that it's all been manageable. It seems the management staff is growing. Recently I found out that I have a young lady managing to build a forest."

Lana: Well that's foresight.

Orazio: How do you mean?

Lana: Well, we're going to have to bury the bodies somewhere.

Carole: Oh Lana, we're burial at sea people.

Both of the ladies laughed. Orazio muttered, "I'm doomed."

Orazio: Lana, I understand that you speak fluent Russian. Where did that come from?

Lana: The Army.

Orazio: Ours or theirs?

Lana: I was a bad girl. I went in the U.S. Army when I was seventeen. It was mutually agreed upon by my parents and the court. I showed an aptitude for language and dishonesty. After Fort Knox, they sent me to Fort Huachuca for counterintelligence training.

Orazio: I thought you had to be twenty one to receive counterintelligence training.

Lana: Did I forget to mention the aptitude for dishonesty?

Orazio: Got it.

Lana: It was they who taught me to be a Ruskie. They gave me interrogation training, weapon training, and lots and lots of close quarter combat training.

Orazio: So you're a trained killer.

Lana: First we talk, then …..

Orazio: Right!

Carole: I'm more interested in hearing how you went into business for yourself.

Lana: Well Carole, we used to go to great length to spy on the Soviets. We listened to their coded messages and intercepted their communication with all kinds of technology. It was interesting, but I found it simpler to just get 'em drunk and get 'em braggin'. My first pimp job was actually for a fag believe it or not. I tried to hustle a guy and he told me he wasn't interested. When I asked why, he told me he needed someone with a bigger cock. Back then it was don't ask don't tell, so the fags had to be more careful. Well, I had a homo in my unit. We all knew, but he was respected. In fact, he was outstanding. I asked him if he wanted the job and he jumped at the chance. Thanked me for appreciating his unique talent and the Russian was thrilled. We knew the Russian would give us a lode of disinformation, but we had become good at reading between the lines. Disinformation always never strays too far from the truth. After that, I started to hunt for girls. There's never a shortage believe me. After a while the army realized the nature of my sources. I actually got a pension from the military, you know, in my real name, whatever that is.

Carole: Did you just drop your old business? I mean, did you fake your death, or what is supposed to have happened to you?

Lana: That Carole, is a very good question. So Svetlana Pavlichenko is here romancing the millionaire. Where is the former lieutenant Janet (Chapstick) Chaplin? You think

94

Chapstick is in reference to my name Chaplin, but really it's in reference to my work with a special stick.

What we did Carole, was to make my whereabouts unknown, but The Ten will keep my action alive as if I were still calling the shots. The mystery of my illusive ability will make me even more formidable, because The Ten will execute action and credit it to me, yet I will never be on the wrong end of the gun. Ghost boss, revenge is impossible, and I can always make a spectacular return; shock and awe baby. I'm almost a legend.

As the car pulled up to the house and into the garage, Lana looked not excited, but unimpressed and resolved.

Carole: So here we are Lana. This is your new home for better or worse. Let's go inside and begin to get you set up. Your luggage will be here soon and you probably want to get into something more comfortable. Obviously you'll want for nothing, but we all know that you're not a lady of leisure and will need some kind of engaging occupation. We want to know if you have any ideas as to where you fit in. We like innovation but not surprises. We know you're vetted by our best, but anytime The Ten is involved ..... well, let's talk.

They went in and Lana went right to the kitchen. She began to look around and pull out the ingredients for what was shaping up to be a steak and rice meal. She was surprised to find that Orazio didn't have much food.

Lana: Nobody cooks here do they?

Orazio: We didn't expect you too.

Lana: You have no salad stuff at all. I'm glad you had these frozen steaks, and this bag of rice. Canned gravy? Ugh. No way.

Orazio: To be frank, I usually get takeout.

Lana: Well, now you have a girlfriend who cooks like a bitch. I shop online, so don't worry about security. Security is something I'm good at. At least I was. Anyway, where's your foil?

Orazio: We have that. Do you want some help?

Lana: God no. Just stay out of my way and nobody will get hurt. Do you have a housekeeper every day? I'll try not to make a mess.

Carole and Orazio looked at each other and nodded. Lana was one of the guys. As they began to set the table and open the wine, Lana asked, "Do you have big plans for me?" Orazio told her they didn't; not at all. They were just happy to harbor her until the threat to her was over. She told them that she had always had such a serious life. She said she wanted to play.

Now Carole and Orazio looked at each other quizzically. "Play?" they asked.

Lana: Yeah, I want to do an idea I've had for a long time. I've seen a lot of relationships as a result of my, we'll call them, interrogation methods. I've seen a lot of men and women get together and listened to them. I've seen a great many patterns that I think people will identify with. I want to make a TV show. You know; a reality show. I know a lot about reality. Do you want to hear about it?

The steaks were seared and the rice was seasoned, buttery, and fluffy. Lana was dishing it up. Carole and Orazio were being pitched. It was a little sneaky. Lana was working them. They loved it. They were in a bit of shock. But, did they want to hear it? Uh, you bet they did.

Orazio: I think we're hearing it already.

Lana: Yes you are. Good catch. Here's how it works. The show is called Bitch Test. It's recorded without the woman knowing it will be a show. The man is an actor.

The premise is a rich man is looking for a lady. He wants the lady to be his mistress, not his potential bride. He is going to pay all of her bills, and is only there for sex, but there is a work agreement.

No Drama, No Bitch.

She must be qualified, pass medical examinations, quarantine for 30 days and be tested again. She must be educated and athletic. In other words, she must have her own life outside of the relationship, but must be quick to be available to him at almost all times. Having children does not disqualify her, but the children are not to know the man. If the children have needs, their needs supersede the man's desires.

Let her sign the agreement and then, we wait to see how long it takes for her to start bitching in violation to the contract.

The man records the times and places of the bitching.

There is no limit to the time it takes for the bitching to start

Once the bitching has occurred for thirty days, the man makes his report on the twelve categories

There are a group of men and women who see the start of the relationship and they bet on how quickly the bitching starts and the extent of it.

We record ten or twelve episodes of Bitch Test and then show it as the one and only season.

The categories are:

1. How long does it take for her to cheat?

2. How long before she accuses him of cheating

3. How long before she leaves clothes at his home

4. How long before she demands more money

5. How long before she talks about her X (or past)

6. How long before she talks about his X (or past)

7. How long before she tells you what her girlfriends think

8. How long before her girlfriends tell you what they think of you

9. How long before she tells you what Oprah thinks

10. How long before she plans your vacations

11. How long before she imposes her family on you

12. How long before she imposes herself on your family

Whoever is closest to guessing the final outcome of the couple's conflicts is the winner.

The man and woman are rewarded for their participation with some kind of compensation as they sign off on the release. Or, they can go on their merry way and receive nothing. There can be no legal consequences to us, as demanding payment for prostitution is regarded with disdain.

Orazio: You have a great deal of experience with this don't you?

Lana: Believe me, this is such a common scenario, I think everybody will see the humor in it.

Orazio: No Lana. We get it, but most people don't have bitchy mistresses. It's certainly dirty enough to capture the imagination of some people, but we're kind of a family values organization so no, we don't want to try to work the bugs out of this idea.

Lana: Well okay, no hard feelings, but what am I going to do?

Carole: Lana, that's my job. I'm our human resources director, and you're both a human and resourceful. You and I are going to pal around together for a while to search for the perfect fit for you. Rige Coos Bay is the land of opportunity. With the drama we're experiencing lately, I think that you will actually give me insight into new possibilities. I think if we keep your tactical ability to ourselves, their just might be a moment when the element of surprise might be an asset that will win a few battles for us that we might otherwise lose. For now, you work in H.R. as my personal assistant. Get to know people and the lay of the land. Anyway, we can use your unique insight. And with you around, women will be less inclined to try to move in on Ratzi.

Lana: Ratzi? Is that what you call him? I like that. And don't you worry about women Carole, with me around, your Ratzi's desire for women will be well taken care of.

Chapter Twelve

Expansion

Orazio was asked for a meeting at his office in Coos Bay with Oscar Rodriguez. It was the first time he had ever asked Orazio for his time. Up to that point, it had always been simple requests for money through Orazio's accountant dedicated to over-see expenditures by Toad. When Oscar asked, he never had to ask twice. Orazio had always been quick to say yes. As the time for the meeting neared, Carole Koslowski arrived at the boss's office. She said that her company was also requested.

Right on time, Oscar burst into the room. He had a big smile on his face. He asked them both to come downstairs with him and out the front door. There, in front of them were their cars. Carole's two seat cotillion white convertible sport car, and Orazio's shockingly deep copper colored two door personal luxury coupe; the Tadpole and the Toad.

Standing behind the cars were the twelve men who had hand-crafted these machines, along with their entire families. Video cameras were recording from every angle. Carole and Orazio looked back and realized that others from the office came out behind them and began to clap. It had only been two years, Orazio had a tear in his eye as he looked, not at the cars, but at Oscar.

As two of the wives came around to open the doors for their investors, Oscar said to Orazio, "*Jefe,* I had to do it this way. I told you from the beginning that I had to make the Toad Ferrari killer, and I did. You knew I was going to give it to Carole, but I couldn't let you be disrespected by blowing you off as first owner. We all love you for the way you just trusted us. We spent a lot of money, and you let us. And your accountant Aurelio, who conspired with us and sometime tricked you a little, the next car goes to him. He never let us down, but he never let you down either. He is the most fair and honest *compañero* from outside the family that we ever worked with. Leonardo said he's like a champion jockey on an unbroken race horse. By the way, he mixed your color when he saw you looking at one of our cars. You said, "Nice color," and that stuck with him. He asked me to mention to you sometime that he wants some horses, but today, it's all about the cars. Congratulations boss.

Orazio said, "I want to see Carole in her car." The top was down, and her Mexican-American lady friends who opened the door helped her in. She looked up at her friends and said, "I want video of every single one of you driving our car." They all nodded. Now, Orazio was surrounded by the guys. Lucas said, "Get your ass in my seat boss. It ain't yours yet; not until you break it in." Orazio looked in at the leather interior. He touched the seat-back with his right hand, and the steering wheel with the left. As he slid onto the seat he noticed that it was a bench seat, not a bucket. He asked, "A bench seat?" Lucas said, "Maybe in this car, you won't be lonely huh? Sometime a bench seat helps you get cozier. And boss, that split back bench is fully reclining. Keep that in mind." Carole opened the passenger side door, dropped herself in and moved over next to Orazio. Everybody clapped and Lucas said, "See. You like that seat now don't you?" and everybody laughed.

Carole and Orazio got out of the cars and noticed that the company tour bus was waiting just down the driveway. Orazio asked, "Are all of you going back in the bus?" Oscar said, "No, I personally drove your car here, and my wife followed me in her Chevelle. She said that she'll never take a bus again. So I'm going home with her.

Orazio: You know Oscar, you never told me why you called the car the Toad.

Oscar: Well boss, you never came to see our band.

Orazio: So?

Oscar: Man, I'm the drummer.

Orazio: So?

Oscar: Well *Mijo*, when you do come to hear us, I'll explain it to you.

Oscar held out his hand. Orazio shook it and thanked him again for the car and the platform to launch the helium battery. It's cool to be a billionaire and have a hero. He loved Oscar Rodriguez.

He and Carole got in their respective cars and drove off down the road. Anything less would have been a disappointment to the real car building visionaries; the guys who built the dream; the guys who wanted the dream experienced, not just gawked at.

*****

Carole and Orazio returned to the office and collapsed. The cars were breath-taking. Silent power and the feeling of unlimited acceleration were nerve-frazzling. Carole told Orazio she wanted to drive his car. He had other ideas.

Orazio got up and walked out to his secretary's office. He said, "Della, get the Blacks in here as soon as you can.

They're in Maryland right now, so whatever time works for them, we'll work around that." He turned to Carole.

Orazio: Among all the vast I.T. guys that we've hired for our insanely custom cyber security, do we have any we can trust?

Carole: I've been keeping an eye on Platt. He's a regular Edward Snowden. He's trying to hack The Ten and The Axis. I don't know how much success he's having, but I do believe that we can trust him.

Orazio: Platt? What's his first name?

Carole: Scott.

Orazio: Get him in here. Does he have a team or does he work alone?

Carole: His Company, Rainforest Software, has thirty one employees but to answer your question, he's got two other guys.

Orazio: Are either of them married?

Carole: These guys? No. They're millennials. They're not too interested in girls. I mean they're not gay, they're just not inclined toward relationships. Remember when the big sign of being media connected was a TV in every room? These guys have keyboards in every room. Girls? They watch porn for ten minutes, relax, and it's back to what they love.

Orazio: Still, I want Lana here when they're here for eye candy.

Carole: Gee, Ratzi, that used to be my job.

Orazio: Yeah well, the voyeur in me wants to watch. I want to watch Lana as much as I want to watch them. Obviously you will watch as well. I don't understand the lack of sex drive in these kids, and I don't believe or can't imagine how it can be. I mean is it their diet, or is it some kind of weird mind control from too much cell phone game microwaves, or what? Let's study this highly unnatural phenomenon. Have too many of them grown up without fathers that now, there's just no man in them? I don't know. Is it suppression of masculine nature from college environment? I wanna watch. Call it a morbid curiosity. The problem is deep. I want my own objective impression.

The Black sisters had their own jet. Even though they were in Maryland, they showed up the next day. Orazio was again astounded by the speed which everything was moving. The resources developed by his conspirators, was always one asset more than he was aware. Of course, they had been flying around the world. Of course they had their own plane. He was impressed. They didn't even make mention of it. They just got it, like you getting a new car. They even got Lana. Just like Oscar Rodriguez, they didn't need permission. They just kicked ass and gave you the results, as if it were all in a day's work.

Orazio had a fancy furnished office with nothing on the desk. That was for the regular visitors. He had a highly functional inner office for the business visitors. He also had a back office, his real office, the office for conspirators. The group was assembled. Orazio, Carole, Della, the Black sisters, Scott Platt, his partners, Jimmy Capasso and Johnny Bencivene, and Lana met in the back-back office.

Orazio: Thank you all for coming. We're going to have some fun. Scott, you and your friends have an interest that is over my head in so far as your artistic level is concerned. I'm a practical man, and consider the computer as a simple tool. You, on the other hand, consider it a world, a beautiful world whose beauty is beyond most people. I am one of those people, I hate to admit it, but you probably consider me to be a Luddite. I respect that. Now, we're going to see if you three are the real deal, or just second string.

Scott Platt: Luddite? No. My mother doesn't know anything about computers and I love her. We don't judge you by our standards. We saw you support that car guy. We saw you support that Chinese kid who created his own monetary system. In fact, supporting that was our favorite thing that you did. We made accounting software for him. He's got his own management style that is a psychological masterpiece in itself. Ryan Chang is more of an economic wizard than Milton Freidman. There's nothing theoretic in his work. It's all practical.

Orazio: What can you tell me about The Axis?

Scott: Axis is Jimmy's hobby. Johnny is working on Main.

Orazio: Main?

Johnny: You don't want to know.

Orazio: Actually Johnny, I need to know everything, but to be practical, maybe not now. Jimmy, what I want is revenge. Some politicians in San .....

Jimmy: Right! The California political crime family messed with your tanker; small potatoes. You won that one. Why the bitch fit?

Orazio: You got it all wrong. My goal is to reform the way governance is conducted in the whole country. California is all bottled up by the political power of an oligarchy. I want to smash that open so my ideas can be evaluated by the people of that State without the election fraud that keeps them in power. Candidates in Cali don't even campaign, they just win. I need vigorous campaigns in order to introduce my methodology to that State.

Jimmy: I'm sorry. I get it. So normally you don't need our help but because you're afraid that The Axis will be called in to jam our geo-fencing techniques, you want us to run herd on them.

Orazio: Something like that.

Jimmy: What do you think Scott? We use this to get them out in the open? We follow the money and use that to possibly find their other sources? Expose their other connections. Expose their superstructure? You see Orazio, people who do what we do have a style. You know Sinatra by his tone and style. We know programmers like that. Also, their motivations or goals give them away. The nature of their game makes it possible for us to imagine what their next move will be.

Orazio: I don't get why you do this.

Scott: It's our game; the real computer game. We don't play Pac Man. Our game is not on the screen. It's in the mind. The real victor is the guy who can operate unimpeded; the guy who can't be messed with while still being able to mess with you. It's just a dominance hierarchy, like with any species in the animal kingdom. The internet is our kingdom. It's cyber war. It's real. If we win, we can literally control and exploit the world. We are the top of the food chain. We can hide anywhere, except from others of our kind. It's stratospheric compared to the meat and potato shit you do. Do you think that we think you're a Luddite? At our level, yes, but we do appreciate that you grow our food. That's a level of productivity we need from you. We appreciate your contribution. We need you, but you bloody well need us, because not all cyber warriors are grounded. We like to think we are the good guys. The Ten are good guys too. Axis and Main are sociopathic. They're burners. We're the god damned fire department, but we're not altruists. We know that's sociopathic too. We do it because we can, and somebody has too, and, as Lao Tzu says, "Though no one listens, the musician plays," it's just our calling. People play poker. The whole world is our poker table. Get it?

Orazio: So if you've got all this dialed, why are you working for me?

Scott: The truth is, you implied that we were going to be tested to see if we were varsity or second string, well honestly, we're the J.V. team. We're just getting off the ground. We're kinda wannabes. We have skills, we've done good work for you, but we are just gathering our resources. The cool part for you is because we are new players to this, we're still kinda disregarded. At this point we're stealth players, and we feel that it's a big part of our game to retain that status. We're not being stalked as prey yet, so we move under the radar. Becoming famous for us almost means it's time to restructure. It's tricky. We may pull off a David and Goliath move. If we do and we crow about it, they'll take us out. The trick is to be self-satisfied. It sucks. There ain't no Rock Star hackers.

Carole: They're being modest. They have a company of thirty one people doing every kind of customer service. They're expanding rapidly. They've gotten themselves in a position where their company runs itself, which is why they can play. They're going to use that company for your geo-fencing and the targeted marketing. Even their own people, as good as they are, are not aware of what Scott, Jimmy and Johnny are up to. Turn them loose Mr. Rige.

Orazio: So you know my goal.

Scott: We assume our role is to have our rank and file do the grunt work while we try to stay on top of The Axis or anybody else your friends hire. We understand what everybody is here for except the new lady. Was it Lana?

Donna Black: Did you ever see Lara Croft Tomb Raider?

Scott: Yeah.

Donna: That's her function.

There was a smile on the faces of all three computer men. Orazio could see that they liked the idea of a "Special Forces Female." He was glad. The addition of that glamour would add the romance for the guys that he wanted.

Scott: Well Lana, I'm glad I asked.

Marla Black: Look boys, we need you to use your geo-fencing technique and your ability to do your target marketing analysis for us. That's essential. I just want to make sure you understand our tactic and what goes on in California.

Scott: What do you mean, "What goes on in California?"

Marla: Let me summarize for everybody and to get my own thoughts straight, and to make sure we all agree. Donna, I'm assuming your recorder is on.

With computer algorithms, the boys will figure out the demographics of the voting region. In addition they will engage in geo-fencing which is to say, they will find groups who use a common Wi-Fi like in a hotel, and bombard them with advertising. Their contact information will be gathered for continued advertising. Through their contacts on their phones and social media, we will get a grip on their inclinations on every issue. Advertising targeted to their sensitivities will manipulate them to support our causes and candidates. This is sleazy, but this is politics. Imagine Carole, something even too dirty for me. Who'd have ever believed it?

Next, California has a voter suppression system called Top Two. The State no longer has political Parties. This has been achieved by controlling the primaries so that in the actual election, one Party has both candidates, and they don't allow another.

The way it works is, most States have a primary where each Party, the Republicans, the Democrats, the Independents, the Libertarians, the Green Party et cetera, send out Party specific primary ballots. Each Party picks its candidate and each party runs someone on the election ballot. In California they have something called Top Two. In that State, at the primary, everybody can vote for anybody, and the "top two" vote-getters are the only candidates on the ballot on the actual Election Day. Few vote in the primary, so the unions, who are stooges for the oligarchy, can pack the primary with its members and put two people on the ballot that they control. On Election Day, the voter is stuck with a forgone conclusion.

With our method, this works in our favor. If we put up three or four candidates who all support each other and vilify the incumbent, we can have the top two, and that is exactly what we are going to do. Your company's demographic research will help a ton and the three of your personal attentions will go a long way to stopping their cyber efforts. You will have perfect cover because you will ostensibly be part of us, not independent agents. Your corporate avatars should be ample insulation from you being identified.

Once our candidates begin, you use our combined candidate swarm, and their agreement with our "Contract with the People," we should be able to overcome their election fraud tactics. Our part, Donna and I, will pound the court to sanitize the voter rolls. We'll run a campaign of vigilance over the Chain of Custody process of the votes. It's a four pronged attack.

Do we all agree?

The room nodded in consensus.

We'll get one Senator in this election and the other one when she comes up in the next and the Governor as well. You know, we have term limits. We have two, four and six year terms for every seat except judges. We just have to smarten up the people so they vote the stinkers out at the end of their term.

Orazio: Carole.

Carole: My job is to find our candidates. I've set up a non-profit in Vallejo to start the process. It's an economically depressed area thanks to closing all the Naval manufacturing that used to go on there. The area will yield the people we need. There are still a lot of over qualified under employed who have an ax to grind against the military cutbacks the Liberal Elite instituted. The devil there has been ready for its due for a long time.

Scott: I haven't seen the non-profit yet. What's it called?

Carole: Well Scotty, my team's all beautiful ladies. We're called The Liberty Belles.

The estrogen in the room was definitely getting to the computer guys. Lana noticed it. So did Orazio. Lana quietly asked Orazio if she could meet with the guys to propose an unrelated idea. Orazio asked, "Is this part of your, 'I want to play' desire?" Lana said, "Funny you should say desire, but yes." Orazio asked, "Just because I'm terrified of your potential to make these guys crazy, will you run it by me first?" She said, "I've been dying to." Orazio said inaudibly, "I'm doomed."

Orazio told Lana, "I'm going to take you and Carole to the Homestead for dinner; we can talk about it there." Lana said back, "If we're going out into the woods I'm going to need to take a big box of Kleenex, sometime I get a little hay fever."

Orazio piped up to the group, "I love it that you're all having fun with this. Is there anything else? No? Okay, thank you all for coming. We all know our jobs. Some of us even seem to have a good grip on each other's jobs. Synergy baby, that's cooperation. Just image if the FBI, the CIA, and the DOJ were able to trust, cooperate and support each other this way. We could all be off making love and art. Now for me, I'm going to go take Carole and Lana to a nice dinner at my friends place in my new car."

Chapter Thirteen

Brothers

The Toad was quiet in such a lovely way as the Orazio, Carole and Lana sped off into the country on their way to the Homestead to have dinner. The scenery and smells were so subliminal in helping all three of them wind down after the intensity of the meeting they had just worked through. Very few words were spoken as they escaped their own minds, and allowed their senses to unfold.

Orazio's Rige Coos Bay Company was a supplier of seafood by the ton, and he always felt good knowing that the delicacy he was eating was the result of a tremendous coordinated effort that included him. Usually he ate poorly. Grab-on-the-go fast food and glorified snacks were not for much more than survival. Food just wasn't a priority for him. Tonight it would be different. Tonight would be Alaskan crab legs or wild salmon prepared with love. Not farmed stuff. Real wild natural creatures captured and cooked just for him and his ladies; truly a feast for a special family. Something to be eaten slowly and savored, not gulped down just in time to restore his blood sugar. He cleared his mind to count his blessings.

Valet? Mr. Rige was mortified. He dropped the ladies off at the front door and parked the car himself. The ladies waited inside, and Robert and Rhonda were descending on them just as the boss walked in. Carole introduced Lana, but Orazio could see that Robert wanted a tour of that car. Out they went. Orazio told them the story. The restaurateurs looked at their friends with real amazement. "So you're going

112

to have an electric car company," Rhonda asked. Orazio smiled and said, "Show them a picture of your car Carole."

Back inside they were seated and their usual chef came right out to the table. They introduced him to Lana and he asked her if she didn't mind him surprising her. She was impressed. He asked her if she had any allergies or aversions. Her awe grew. The car, the place, the host and his wife, the chef, the considerate treatment of everybody by Rige, and the reciprocal considerate treatment by everybody toward Rige was kinda fairytale. She felt a real sense of rock solid stability or could it have been the intangible feeling of "home?" She smiled back the chef and said, "You're going to prepare a memory for me aren't you? I'd love it."

Irresistibly, focus was on the food. The three just abandoned the complexity of their thoughts for the simple luxury of an atmosphere, perfect in every detail. Once the food was finished, and the blackberry brandy was arriving for dessert, Lana said she had an idea.

Lana: Listen guys, I keep thinking about those computer geeks. They're all single. Their whole company only has one married guy. Aren't there any geekettes? I think guys like that could really enjoy something that may seem a little socially incorrect but hear me out.

Half asleep, Ratzi and Carole were vulnerable.

You know my nickname in the service was Chapstick right? It doesn't refer to lip balm. When I turned twenty-one, the guys who took interrogation training with me gave me a surprise party. They really busted my balls because I was a girl, really an under-aged girl who had survived what nobody even took seriously at first. I really got my ass kicked and earned the

113

respect of that very special band of brothers. I told you we had a wink-wink secretly gay guy in the squad and that guy earned their respect too. What I didn't tell you about that guy, which only even made his "difference" harder, was that he was British, at least as a kid. Some of the guys called him Bond, Jane Bond.

At the party, I got a lot of joke gifts, as you can well imagine. In England, they call men Blokes or Chaps. Well, Jane Bond gave me a big purple dildo called the Chapstick. Get it? That branded me with that name, Janet "Chapstick" Chaplin. Even may name Janet was like Jane, like Jane Bond. Believe me it was the most fraternal confirmation for both of us you can imagine.

Well, I never told anybody, but as it turned out, I loved the thing. I used it a lot. It was like the love-cock of my whole crew. I fantasized about all of them. I realized that women did this forever. I mean, not you Carole, there's no way you're frustrated. *ppppp.....* but I did. So I got to thinking, I know men jerkoff all the time, so where's their appliance? Then I learned about the sex dolls. Not the creepy blowup dolls; the lifelike robot girls. Every guy should have one. I mean not you Ratzi, there's no way you're frustrated. *ppppp .....* but for everybody else. Think of it as a dildoette.

I can see that you're both mortified, but let me continue. Guys like Scott, Johnny and Jimmy get up in the morning probably with a hard on. I don't know how they deal with it, but I can imagine. Some mornings you're busy, but some mornings you have a little extra time. Same in the shower, there's the in and out one, and the "let's hit all the potential" one. I mean, sometime a guys just gotta do what a guys' gotta do. With technology, it could be better.

114

Just imagine, Scott wakes up. He's aroused. Normally, he'd fuck the mattress, but now he reaches over and finds a very lifelike little ass. He rubs his cock on it, rolls it over and nails it, right in the self-lubricated, automatic pulsating pussy. In ten minutes, he's a whole new man. I think he'd love it. For me, sometime I just can't get to sleep until I play with my big plastic vibrating lubricated love toy.

What do you think Carole? Can the boys handle a meeting with me over this? I won't even consider it without your blessing. I don't want to interlope if there are business concerns. I'm just a girl trying to relieve a little stress and loneliness, and help my fellow man.

Carole: Well, that's a level of compassion you don't hear every day.

Lana: Carole, there are all different levels of fantasy and utility with these things. Look, we have Alexa and Siri to interact with. Some of these dolls can play chess with you. These guys like video games. Computer game, computer chick. One that can stay up all night with you. A computer friend who can do research with you, who can get to know you. A computer listener who can remember every word you ever say; who can visually record everything "she" sees and plays it back for you. Talk about a photographic memory. "Honey, where are my keys?" Computer Babe, "You left them in the right front pocket of the pants you came home in. The pants are currently in the wash basket."

Who wouldn't want that? And if you get horny, you can get "service" from a machine that can interact with you in a variety of sexy vocal accents. Ah, if only my Chap could talk.

Carole: You know Lana, I was always curious as to what happened to the man in your life when you assumed the new identity. Am I out of bounds in asking?

Lana: Me? A man? No. I work alone, even in bed. Sex for me is putting a guy on his back and fucking the secrets out of him. I can't even climax until I have all of his PIN numbers, and then really I still don't. I'm strictly hardware, no software. Don't worry about me. Probably eventually a psychiatrist will con me out of my pants, but until then. I'm just like one of those geeks; just not emotionally available.

Now, I know that neither one of you would be interested in something like this; you're far too satisfied with the way things are for you. *ppppp* ..... No, this is for the guys. I'm sure they know all about these dolls; probably know the builders. Maybe they even have them, maybe they're afraid to, but maybe a little barrier breaking endorsement, maybe a little permission as it were from a hot bitch like me just might be all they need to explore technology in a, let's call it, "user friendly" way, that taboos may have slowed their prioritizing of this particular domestically comforting medium.

Orazio said, "Lana, that was an amazingly eloquent display of bullshit, really great." Lana said, "It was from the heart." Orazio said, "*Ppppp* .....Carole, green light?" She stammered back, "Yeah." Orazio said, "Okay, you got it." Lana said back, "Well, thank you both. You are a couple of real humanitarians. I'm feeling like I'm ready to head home, can we go?"

On the way to the restaurant, Orazio drove, Carole was right up next to him, and next to her on the front seat was Lana. This time, Lana jumped in the back seat. Carole sat in the front, but all the way over by the door. There wasn't much chit-chat. Lana asked if Orazio could drop her off at the house on the way to dropping off Carole. She said she wasn't used to eating and drinking as they had, and felt suddenly tired and wanted to go right in and take a few Naproxens.

Orazio pulled up to the house and Lana said good night and thanks, and ran in. She said silently to herself, "You monkeys owe me."

Forty-five minutes later Lana looked out the window to see that the car hadn't moved. She said quietly to herself, "I bet you're glad I left you that box of Kleenex."

The next morning the car was gone. Orazio showed up at work a few minutes after ten; Carole, a little after lunch.

*****

Alejandro Vasquez nicknamed Jando, who assembled the bodies for the Toad had a son named Lucas, named after his friend Lucas who did the car's interiors. Lucas was the favorite computer code writer of Bobby Diez. Lucas had created a computer game called "*Mine.*" The basic idea was to find material in space, mine it for water and minerals, and build a space colony. The reality was to actually find stuff out in real outer space, the fantasy was how to live in, and propel the mining ship to go get it.

Lucas had begun to play the game with Murray Atkins, a bar tender who lived near the Jet Propulsion Laboratory (JPL) out in Pasadena California. Murray was just a real regular guy who was interested in physics and decided to take courses through the computer with the University of Utah. They had an excellent program that even offered a PhD in atomic and molecular physics, and though it was really only his hobby, he felt that there was nothing more important than

117

following through on his intuition. Somehow, to him, subatomic particle theory seemed reasonable. He had a few theories of his own. If his ideas were visionary, he needed to know. He recognized himself in the analytic nature of the young man's game. The kid was like him. Vision and dreams that reached far beyond his ability to gather the resources he needed to follow through with necessary multi-billion dollar experiments.

Murray began to correspond with Lucas, describing his ideas for propulsion in space. Lucas told Bobby Diez about the ideas, and Bobby began to monitor the contact. It wasn't long before Bobby told Lucas's father that his son was writing with an adult, but the adult was not a problem. Alejandro looked over his son's shoulder for a couple of nights and asked Bobby, "What do you think?" Bobby said, "I think get Murray together with Mr. Rige." Lucas agreed.

Murray was shocked to find out that Lucas had told the men about their conversations, he hadn't even considered that the communication might be inappropriate, but did understand that Lucas was just a kid. "Just a kid," Murray said. "That kid is an explorer itching to go forth into the unknown. Don't sell him short. Sure, he's got a long way to go, but because he's got a long way to go, we better get started. He needs to go to M.I.T. like right now.

Bobby and Jando invited Murray up to Bend to meet with Lucas. They offered him a plane ticket, a place to stay, and when he arrived, they picked him up with the Toad limo. That's how he ended up in Oregon. They got a good feeling about the man. Orazio was surprised to get the call from Alejandro and Bobby. He was impressed by the groundwork they had done vetting Murray's worth. He asked if Carole

118

could go get him and bring him in. They knew Carole, so they smiled knowingly, and that's how Murray ended up in Mr. Orazio Rige's office.

There he was, feeling confident because he felt he had Carole on his side, not knowing that everybody else felt the same way. He felt fortified by her as opposed to alone on a battlefield. He felt unabashed when he told the Billionaire his scheme.

Murray Atkins told Orazio Rige, "Sir, if you want real power, you have to hold the high ground. If you're up on the mountain where no one can get at you, you're invulnerable. The problem is the high ground now is outer space. But space is great. Space is a very sanitary place, a very exclusive place. I see that you want to manage society, to insulate it from petty human frailty. Doing that here on Earth is necessary because it is the only place we have to live. We do need to build a fortress here, but all castles are ultimately vulnerable. When the chateau strong-hold finally falls, every Chatelaine always has to have an escape route. Life on Earth seems fragile to me. We have so many paths to apocalypse. The problem is, escape has not been practical, but maybe now it is.

I was watching dolphins play, and the idea hit me.

The way the system works is this:

The Earth has a magnetic charge, it's why compasses work.

The reason the Earth has a charge is because the center of the Earth is a giant rotating mass of iron. Magnets are made of iron.

If you reverse the rotation of the Earth, the poles will reverse.

This is true of the Alternator in your car, and is true of all electric motors.

At the atomic level, particles have an electromagnetic charge.

For example, Protons have a positive charge, and electrons have a negative charge.

There are other subatomic particles, but we can use those two of the most well-known for the sake of illustration.

In the subatomic realm, there is another important entity to introduce. That is the photon. The photon does not have a charge, it is understood as a tiny packet of energy, traveling at the speed of light, more or less looking for a target. This is how sunlight warms you. Light is made of photons.

Protons and electrons have a charge because they spin. My assumption is that if they have the same mass but spin the opposite way, they become an antiproton or an antielectron, in short, particles of antimatter, particles of the same mass but with reversed charge. We all pretty much accept that if matter finds antimatter, both particles are annihilated, releasing their energy. Needless to say we're glad there is not an abundance of antimatter.

Apparently, they all spin the same way, so no big boom.

So you ask, how do these understandings help us?

We want to launch and travel in space. It's the destiny of humanity.

Our problem is, now, we do this by burning rocket fuel, as if space travel is going to be done in a great big Cadillac. Well, there ain't no V8 rockets. No, rockets are not the answer. It's ancient Chinese technology. Probably the last thing they invented before they based their technological advancement on intellectual property theft. Yeah, I have issues, but I'm dealing with them.

There are forces that we know about, other than explosions. We all know that escaping gravity is a huge challenge. It's why we have zillion megaton rockets, but we're done with that.

We all know that magnetism is a much greater force than gravity. The entire gravity of the Earth is less than an electromagnetic crane in a junkyard. So how do we employ magnetism?

We know that opposite poles attract and like poles repel, so we create an environment where the positively charged launch base on Earth repels the positively charged space ship, making that baby jump right off the table so to speak; right off into space if we charge it enough.

The problem is of course, like with all magnets, as soon as the magnet can, it will flip over and now the unlike poles will be facing each other. This will make the space ship come back to Earth hard and fast; disaster.

So how do we control that?

Now comes the tricky part.

The life of an atom is extremely short; millionths of a second before its components fly off to combine with other particles, or emit or absorb energy. It's a busy little place. Atoms with a balance of positive and negatively charged particles are stable, but these subatomic particles spend a lot of their time in an unstable, or let's call it an "unassigned" period. You can be an electron that is not part of an atom.

Each of the uncountable number of subatomic particles has their own tiny magnetic field. All of these particles have the same direction of rotation, west to east, for positive; east to west for negative, but rotate on a different axis. These axes are completely random. That is why they don't create a unified field. It's zillions of little fields that "cancel each other out" in our perception.

If you could line them up; get them to have a unified axis, they would not only create a unified field, but that field would grow on itself through a cascade of magnetically cooperating particles. This cascade concept was why some scientists thought that one atomic bomb would continue to have a reaction that would never end until all matter was destroyed. We're all glad they were wrong. We have controllable nuclear power, and are not annihilated.

But how do we line the subatomic particles up and control the direction of cascade?

To make this work, we had to make an assumption. If we were wrong, the invention wouldn't work. If the invention did work, it wouldn't mean that our assumption was correct, but it would give us evidence that it might be. The invention might work for an unknown reason that we would one day find, but for us, we would just be glad that it worked.

The assumption was the ether.

When you throw a rock into water, the waves that occur are the water lining up in response to the energy of the impact. These waves can be so strong that waves of water coming off a big boat are able to support a surfer. He can travel on them. In fact, dolphins commonly surf on ship wakes. They understand this, as now, so do I!

Our assumption was that subatomic particles exist in a medium that we call ether, like really thin water, something so thin that we cannot detect it, but in their micro world, it's their ocean. If the ether is hit with a stream of magnetically charged particles, energized and directed by photon bombardment (an energized proton blast), it would generate a wake. Being magnetic it would turn the subatomic particles to a unified axis as they lined up with the ensuing field, creating a self-propagating stronger and stronger electromagnetic field as it grew. This would be done behind the ship to repel it, while being done in from of it to attract it. It would be pushed from behind and pulled from the front. This would create the necessary magnetic stability. A wave has a high point and a low point, a positive moment and a negative moment. The ship would use both, propelled by one, and drawn by the other.

These particles react in millionth-of-a-second intervals. The timing of the alternating process is quick for us, but an eternity for them. The ship would move with a smoothness that if Max Planck's constant is correct, couldn't be smoother.

Realize, we have alternating current in our homes. This idea works.

The cascade would simply dissipate when the energized particle bombardment was stopped or colloquially, when we turned off the light.

The ship would pass through the ether of space this way, being pushed and pulled. Since there is very little to stop the inertia of the ship in the ethereal void of space, even pushed or pulled by one particle would be compelling, and promote acceleration. Direction of the ship would be easily achieved by directing the light beam to change the direction of the wake.

Full stop would also be easily achieved by reversing the direction of the wake.

The energy source is inexhaustible. One thing that we can always depend on is that the universe is full of light, and if that changes, propulsion is the least of our problems.

To begin the testing, we're going to need electricity. I understand you have a geo-thermal power plant. Maybe, we should start to think about another one. Next we need a quiet, out of the way location near the plant. I'm thinking Brothers. Thirty to fifty miles south of Prineville on Rt. 20 and maybe a mile or two off the highway near Brothers Oregon just seems to be calling for its fate. There's a model rocket launch range out there already. It's perfect.

Do you have any snacks?"

Orazio looked at him. Carole said she'd get him something from the cafeteria. Murray thanked her and looked at her to see if he still had her approval. She gave him just enough wink and nod to let him know that he hadn't blown it.

Orazio said, "Brothers?" Murray said, "It's already almost a mile high. Compared to launching from Florida, the first mile toward space is free. Brothers has almost no weather and all the sand you can add to your concrete is right at your feet. The location is like I like my women, cheap and discrete."

Orazio asked, "What is the chance of success with your idea?" Murray told him he didn't know. It would be a totally new field. Orazio thought, did this half-goofy dreamer just make an electromagnetic field joke? He asked, "Can we make a small demo and work our way up before the need for another geo-thermal power plant?"

Murray knew he had captured Orazio's imagination. He said, "I'm going to need very little to start, but as I get good results, the needs will become great. The good news is the up-front part should be not just cheap, but conclusive. To be honest, we may run into insoluble problems quickly, killing the whole thing. You're going to gamble on an unqualified physicist, but if you win, it's better than any lottery you could ever play. If we lose, we'll at least patent everything so that if someone smarter than me comes along and perfects this thing, we might still be able to get licensing money or some other benefit, you know, like a Nobel Prize."

Orazio said, "Okay Mr. Atkins, what I do is to assign an accountant to watch over your expenditures. If you can justify your needs to my man, he'll provide liberally. If you get carried away, he'll rein you in. Bring you back to Earth so to speak." Murray smiled at the joke and said, "One more thing, as much as his father allows, Lucas Vasquez is one of us." Now Rige smiled. Loyalty! The men shook hands.

Chapter Fourteen

The Only Things Worth Doing

"You're building a rocket base?" Scott Platt asked. Orazio banged his hand on his desk. "How is it that everybody knows everything I do?"

Scott: Look Mr. Rige, your security is part of our job. When we saw the guy come to your office, we wondered who he was. We got his identity with facial recognition software. We easily found his video game history with Lucas Vasquez and went about reading their email correspondence. We saw him leave your office and pump his fist outside your door. We knew, more or less, what his proposal was and that it must have been successful; simple deduction.

Orazio: Scott, do you read my correspondence?

Scott: No. Your office computers are encrypted. We can't get in. Atkins, on the other hand is an open book. We're concerned about The Axis or Main picking up on this. Nothing anybody has done should have drawn their attention, but you never know.

Let me tell you a little something about my friends. I'm the guy here on Earth who wants to make a better world. Jimmy and Johnny have other interests in addition to our common one. Both of them are of the firm belief that space science and medical science are the only things worth doing. They believe that the future of our species is in the colonization of the infinite real estate of space. They believe that in addition to working that out, a complete understanding of our physiology and brain, or brains if you include the intestinal track are essential to the kind of longevity necessary to adapt us to the

126

disregard of mortal time and circadian rhythm that will be experienced as space colonization evolves, and the twenty-four hour day fades like a vestigial organ into our planetary past.

Please understand, we are not talking about a near-Earth orbiting thing. We are talking about a vast synthetic home that is leaving and never returning. It will have its own completely unique culture, completely devoid of contact with our old planetary life. It will be a culture not searching for another planet to inhabit, but quite the contrary, its people will regard planetary life with its weather and insect bites and random viral and microbial infestations to be icky.

Jimmy Capasso is dedicated to being among the first to leave, and Johnny Bencivene wants to be there as his doctor. In short, if you understand planning to leave the Earth, we have a medical research proposal that we'd like to discuss with you. This is not really in my purview; it's more the two of them. One thing you need to know about us, we don't do our research in a lab like Thomas Edison. We read everything that's going on around the world and try to connect dots. There is a ton of research that is redundant because of politics. That's stupid. If knowledge was shared, progress would be far quicker, but people, government, is covetous of their little breakthroughs, so everybody has to keep making the same ones separately as if they're ground-breaking at each time and in each place.

We think we have "pirated" enough research from all over and connected it in a way that no one else has. One of the problems with life in space, just one, but it is a big one is fighting radiation. You really can't stay there without considerable shielding. We're approaching the problem from a completely different angle. I want Johnny to explain it to you.

Orazio: When?

Scott: When do you think?

Orazio nodded.

Scott picked up his phone, "Johnny, can you join us in Mr. Rige's office?"

Johnny: Sorry Scott, Jimmy and I had to leave. Get Rige and come over to our remote location right now, we got the sub.

Scott: Mr. Rige, you don't want to miss this. Let's go.

Orazio follows on the heels of Scott Platt having no idea what the hell was going on. As they got into Scotts car, he said, "The guys have located The Axis in their Indian Submarine."

Orazio: So what are they going to do?

Scott: They're going to launch a missile from North Korea at it.

Orazio: WHAT?

Scott: Yeah, we've had this capability for over a year. We figured it out. You know, the launch code. The sub must be in range. They must be working with Japan. This is going to be great.

Orazio: You're going to murder people?

Scott: No no no no no, the missile is unarmed. We're just going to lob it into the ocean near them. The incident will be considered harmless by the United Nations as just an unarmed missile test. They don't know about the submarine. The perplexed North Korean government will never admit that something out of control happened, but The Axis will shit.

Orazio: Won't this be tracked back to us?

Scott: No, the command code for this will be sent from an uninhabited atoll and the apparatus will self-destruct immediately after the command is received. We're not beginners.

The men arrive at the computer lab, built into a motorhome about a mile north of the Coos Bay office. Scott says, "Mobile unit," as they go inside and Johnny and Jimmy are smiling ear to ear.

Johnny: Look Scott, there they are.

Scott: How do you know it's them?

Johnny: They surfaced to charge their batteries. Too bad they don't have our batteries huh?

Scott: No, the sub is nuclear. It's got plenty of energy. It must have surfaced to get food. It's got its own capacity to make air and water. God, look at it, just sitting there on the surface. Did you see a supply ship leave? Wait, no, the supply ship is still coming. Oh, let's let it get a little closer. How did you find them in the first place?

Jimmy: My algorithm got 'em. I've got a computer watching surfacing vessels. This boat doesn't exist.

Scott: But there it is. Go ahead Jimmy, launch.

Jimmy pressed the button, and they watched.

Orazio: What's happening?

Scott: Keep watching.

After about three minutes, the submarine submerged and the supply ship reversed course.

Orazio: Is that it. I still don't understand.

Scott: Keep watching.

About four or five minutes later, the missile entered the screen and splashed down harmlessly in Empty Ocean. The three men cheered, "Well that ought to keep them 'em on their toes huh, Scottie?" Jimmy said.

Orazio: I can't believe you did that.

Scott: Uh, did what? I don't see anything.

Johnny: So, Mr. Rige, did you want to see us about something?

*****

Scott and Orazio returned to Scott's car and followed the motorhome out onto Route 540. Just up on Commercial Street they came to a two story building surrounded by truck trailers. Orazio asked, "Where are we?" Scott said, "Our house."

A big steel garage door rose, and the motorhome went in. Scott parked his car near the office door. A big sign on the door that said, "Rainforest Trucking LLC," instructed visitors to contact "John" at the posted phone number for an appointment. He offered to Orazio to come on in. Inside was a small reception room with no one behind the inner office window. Once through those doors, they were joined by Johnny and Jimmy who gestured to a set of stairs.

Upstairs was their home, a large room with big convex skylights. There was computer stuff all over the place, and a half dozen black fabric recliner chairs. Over at one work station was a man reading a screen. Along the walls were kitchen amenities. Also were open doors that led to spacious bed rooms. On the wall was a poster that read, "Hard Work Matters."

Johnny immediately grabbed some food and went to a computer station. Jimmy brought Orazio a bottle of Coca Cola and said, "Have a Coke and a smile," and parked next to Johnny and lit up his own screen.

Orazio said, "I've always wanted a place like this, but I never had the relationships with people that made it make sense. You guys just don't care about traditional life do you?"

Scott: Jimmy takes care of his sister and her two kids. That's his family.

Orazio: Where is the father of those kids?

Scott: Killed in the Middle East. Don't bring it up. Johnny takes care of his parents and his handicapped brother. That's his family. And I take care of them, they're my family. This place is what we need. Our employees have no reason to come to a work location. They're all programmers who work from the place of their choosing. Everybody has different circumstances, so why force them into a barn. Hell, some of them don't even have cars. Our world is not like your world, not like it at all.

131

We don't care if they're fat or skinny, Asian or Caucasian, young or old, men or women, we only want capability. We don't care if they speak other languages or have ethnic backgrounds. We only want lucid expedient completion of tasks. We pay for results. We allow broad latitude in our expectations because we have a good idea as to the capacity of the person to whom we assign each task. We are ability coordinators.

It's like the sign you saw on our front door, Rainforest Trucking. That business belongs to John Kupski, not Johnny Bencivene. John's business is somewhat like yours. He directs independent owner/operators with truck tractors to truck trailers that need to get somewhere. He has a trucking company but owns no trucks. The trailers you see outside are ones that operators somehow got stuck with. John recovers abandoned trailers and shipping containers and sells them as a sideline.

Pointing to the man reading the computer screen, Orazio asks, "Is that him there?"

Scott: No Mr. Rige, that man is what makes me, sorta' like you. That's my STEM kid. That's why we brought you here, to meet Sammy Zane. Dr. Zane is the discovery of Jimmy. Jimmy is interested in medical science. He got into what you would call "a chat room" with about ten guys interested in epigenetics. After reading the doctors and dilatant researchers' discussions, he realized that Sammy over there was special, so he brought him here.

Sammy doesn't need test tubes and white lab coats. He needs large scale computational power. He needs to be able to store and process massive amounts of data. So we provided it. I'm going to let Jimmy introduce you to him. Hey Jimmy.

Jimmy came over and laughingly reported the scramble that was going on over North Korea and its surprise missile test. Japan was screaming. China was posturing. America was threatening sanctions and the United Nations was condemning the Jews. He imagined that The Ten, knowing they didn't fire the missile, would assume it was done by Main. Main would assume it was The Ten. The Axis wouldn't be sure what happened, but they would be preoccupied for a few days, and still need their supplies.

Jimmy called out, "Hey Sam." Sammy Zane looked up and stood up. He raised his arms over this head and stretched. Jimmy gestured to Orazio to go to him and they walked over. Sammy looked into Orazio's eyes and asked, "How do you feel?" Orazio was surprised by the question. He just said, "Fine."

Jimmy introduced them, "Orazio Rige, Doctor Samuel Zane. Sambo, Ratzi Rige." Sammy shook Orazio by the shoulders and said, "You look healthy, that's good. On your way here I read-up on you, you have, at least in the press, an impressive resume. The guys told me the press only touches the surface with you, they said we could trust you so I will. I hope you can trust me."

Orazio: I hope so too. Apparently you're going to show me something that's going to be hard to take. Whatta ya got?

Sammy Zane: What I got is the right question, and hopefully the right answer. The question needs to be, what are we really?

We look at ourselves as we stand before the mirror and think, that's me.

But is the reflection you see there all of you? No, it's merely the outside.

So you go deeper. Your organs, your skin, your brain, is that you, or are you governed by your gut when it wants food, or your sex drive when it wants? Is that you?

So you go deeper. Your stomach and digestive system breaks down food into its chemical components and your lungs absorb oxygen for the oxidation reduction reactions that create energy so your cells can grow, function, and reproduce. Is that all you are?

So you go deeper yet. Nucleotides are organic molecules that form for a reason that at this point can only be imagined as a random happenstance. Nucleotide molecules are the basis of all life on Earth. Your cells are as dependent upon them as you are on your heart, lungs and digestive track. Are we just the evolution of random molecular structures? Is that all we are?

These molecules are nothing more than atomic and subatomic particles and tiny packets of energy interacting with each other at speeds, millions of times per second. The very nature of these particles and energy is completely incomprehensible to our sensory perception.

Is that all of what we are?

Here on Earth, we don't realize that we actually live in space because the Earth we perceive living on is actually an organic spaceship. We think we live on Earth, and we do, but we also actually live in space too. We're evolved to live in our environment. Now, we want to move out. We want to live in the rest of space, but we're not able to adapt naturally, so we need to ask ourselves, can we do it through technology?

Well, to do that experiment, it's important to know what we are.

We are an organism that is viable, so we have to start there. If you take a car that runs well at sea level and drive it two miles up into the mountains, you will have to adjust its engine for the thin air or it won't function well. You can do it because you know how the engine works. So, to colonize space, we need to know how we work, because we will have to adapt to that environment. We put on clothes to work in hostile weather. We will have to "suit-up" for the hostility of our new place.

The key is, we need to maintain us, and keep us running, and keep us reproducing.

So we start at the beginning.

You take a healthy guy. He's built of zillions of cells and loaded with chemicals communicating with electrochemical reactions. That is where survival for us lives. Right there!

Those chemical molecules make up the basic building plans that are the basis of who we are or what we are. Those construction plans are referred to as DNA and RNA. I'm sure you've heard of DNA, am I right?

Orazio: Of course.

Sammy: Now, the DNA is a chain of plans. Each thing that you're made of is specified in that chain. Bone cells, brain cells, blood cells, skin tone, height, body type, how big your nose is, propensity for things like cancer or a variety of diseases, are all determined by that chain of plans.

When you're born, that chain is exactly who you are. If you are born healthy, you will never be healthier or "more you" than you are at that moment. That chain must remain intact for you to stay that way for each cell and each kind of cell to reproduce properly. The problem is, everything that happens to you affects that chain. Sunshine breaks the chain or twists it. Everything you eat damages the chain to some tiny degree. Pollution in the air you breathe does the same. And the biggest, baddest, DNA killer of them all is radiation, like from the Sun, but could also be from microwaves in the air, like the ones zooming in and out of your cell phone. All of these contaminants mutate your cells as they reproduce.

You are not the person who was born back years ago. You are a mutant. You are damaged. Eventually the damage will result in your body creating cancer cells. Cancer cells are cells that you're creating in your body that are not part of the plan that your DNA had for you when you were born. We all have some small or large amount of cancer, some benign, some malignant; some reproducing quickly, some slowly.

There are plenty of other problems with mutating cells in your body. I just picked cancer because it's easy to understand. Even weird stuff growing on your skin is a sign of this break down. Some see it as natural aging, but aging is a colloquial term. A great many ailments associated with aging can be truthfully just you mutating to death.

Well, there is a lot of radiation in space. It's a problem. There are other problems, but most of them are just mechanical. For me, illness, "aging," or mutation from radiation is the focus of my work.

So what do we do? Think of it this way.

Say you have a machine, a car let's say, and you have a service manual for that machine. You should be able to maintain the machine forever. Now say that each week, someone either removes or changes one word in the manual.

After a while the machine gets harder and harder to maintain. Maybe you start using the wrong viscosity of oil, or you make incorrect adjustments. Maybe you install a part improperly or replace it with a wrong part altogether. One day, you won't have enough information to keep the damn thing running. It dies, and there's nothing you can do. But what if before you die, someone brings you a perfect copy of the original manual? You can bring the machine back up to spec.

What I proposed and am perfecting is maintaining the manual. When you are born, we take serious samples of your DNA. We keep your specific plans on file. Now, each year, we bring you in for a checkup. You have natural anti-bodies. Anti-bodies are your own body's blood warriors that search, identify and destroy virus or bacterial cells that your body doesn't like, foreign cells, cells that aren't you. They cure you when you're sick. The trouble is, they don't know everything. The other trouble is, once you mutate, the mutated cells are the new you as accepted by the anti-bodies, so they stay.

What I have created is anti-bodies that have the original plans. My anti-bodies are given to your DNA chain and will search, identify, and destroy any cell, including an invading disease cell, but more importantly, a cell that you create that is not consistent with your original DNA. Anything that's not you when you were born will be killed and flushed out of your body through normal elimination.

You are as healthy as when you were born, but you are not a baby. The normal function of the pituitary gland that brings you into maturity does not change. You grow up; you just don't grow into a mutant. Theoretically you shouldn't die of "old age," but the thought of that is inconceivable. I'm not trying to sell you on immortality here, in fact, since there is absolutely no clinical study on this whatsoever, I'm not making any claim. All I'm saying is we need to try this.

Orazio: My God. You're talking about the need for this in space travel, but what about right here right now? My God, I mean, does it have to be a baby? Can you do this with a healthy grown-up and prevent or cure cancer? I mean, I'm starting to need glasses. Can you make it where I don't get worse? My God, what is the limit of this? How can we test it?

Sammy: Well big boy, we're testing it now, at the least the four of us are.

Orazio: You mean the four of you have been sampled and …..

Sammy: Right. We could never take this to the FDA. Can you imagine the whole mess ….. I mean look what the stem cell people went through. We don't have time for their ethical debate and bureaucratic bullshit.

Orazio: How long has this "testing" been going on?

Sammy: Yeah, we took the samples a year and a half ago. We went through an extremely intense physical examination. The trouble with us is we're in pretty good shape. So anyway, we waited a year and injected ourselves with the anti-bodies. We didn't have enough disease for any appreciable revelations in our day to day life, but we suffered no ill effects. We believe it's at least, totally safe.

Obviously we can't ask a parent to donate a child and we would never administer this test to anyone involuntarily, but we're getting ready to begin to prospect for volunteers. Obviously, it would have to be done extremely cautiously.

Orazio: How do you "teach" the anti-bodies what to do?

Sammy: That explanation would take a tremendous background in immunology, and then, I'd have to, as the saying goes, I'd have to kill you. I own this; we own this I should say.

Jimmy: No Sammy, this is credited to you. We know our part in this development, but you are the genius on this one. One day you could have done this yourself, but we could never have done this without you, no, you're the man here, we're just your grunts.

Sammy: We'll sort that out later, in the meantime, this is, let's say "Private Property," and it's only protection is secrecy.

Chapter Fifteen

Facing Up

Orazio returned to his office at his shipping company to consider the labyrinth of ideas that he had been fed far too quickly over the past several years. Genetic manipulation, space ships, space colonization, world changing batteries charged with geothermal energy, crazy computer hackers, sex robots, it was all too much.

He needed to sit quietly and reflect. He asked himself, what did he really want? So much was happening. Everybody was working effectively because they were unbridled from bureaucracy. His dream was happening, and because it was happening, it was bigger than the management by his patronage. The STEM kids were flying. He was out of his league. Even he, bigshot Orazio Rige, was being blown away by the next generation. He loved it. All they had needed was freedom. He provided the freedom that a parent provides a young developing child. A well raised child does not worry where his next meal is coming from. He moves forward. That's freedom; the freedom to have an unencumbered mind, the freedom that comes from faith in your security. That's what the government is supposed to provide. That's what the originators of our Constitution had envisioned and planned. It was not lost on him that it was their gift by example to the world, and what he was doing was the gift in-kind to an America that had lost its way.

He decided to just sit in his office, take off his tie, look out the window, and maybe just fall asleep in his big leather chair.

No such freakin' luck. Marla and Donna Black came busting in like ready to party.

Marla Black: Well Ratzi, we knew it was coming. The three letter agencies are all over us. Even Lana couldn't back them off. It's the good old tax evasion gambit. They're coming after you Al Capone style. They're so unimaginative; they're using 1920's Elliot Ness tactics? It's an insult.

Orazio: So why are you smiling?

Donna Black: Why? We're ready; been ready. We've anticipated this. They think they have us but they don't. They're in such disarray that they will never get a consensus as to how to proceed against us. Their system is just too top heavy and bottom sloppy. We're moving forward too fast for them with their lazy ineptness for them to catch up. We're gonna outrun 'em.

Orazio: You have a plan?

Donna: It's all media. The Ten are going to make you a national hero. They're going to pound the American people with propaganda that will make it difficult for the media-worried politicians to know the best course of action. They'll balk.

Orazio: Why are The Ten going to do this? What's their game?

Donna: Good, you get it. The Ten want The Axis to be hired by the government for their counter-attack. The government is a bunch of disorganized juveniles who have no computer savvy. The partnership will be bad for The Axis. There will be Congressional oversight hearings and boondoggles like that. The government has too many stupid people in it. They always

141

make a mess. The Axis, in frustration, will have to leave them high and dry. The Ten are hoping that it will be the downfall of The Axis or at least the kneecapping, as it were.

Marla: We're going to get together with you and Koz and write a speech that will vault you into national superstardom.

Orazio: How much time do we have?

Marla: Plenty. If there is one thing you can depend on the government for, it's delays.

Orazio: You know what, I don't want a delay. I understand exactly what I have to do. I know exact what I want to say. Who am I going to be facing?

Marla: There is an IRS office in Salem that we can use as a venue.

Orazio: I want it televised.

Marla: I don't know if they'll do that.

Orazio: Have The Ten do it no matter what anybody says. I want everybody in America to see me stand against the Swamp. I'm no actor, but this is the role I'm destined to play. It's my place in all this. Though I did not want this, and my original intention was innocent, this is what they've compelled me to do, and do it I will.

Marla: Orazio? … Ratzi?

Orazio: Get Carole. I need all three of you. We need to record this. I want every word of every suggestion kept for consideration. I've anticipated this confrontation ever since they hijacked my oil tanker. Now, I'm gonna give 'em my response.

Orazio Rige arrived at the IRS building in response to their demand for a deposition. He brought along his two lawyers and a half a dozen witnesses.

They informed him that his testimony was going to be recorded. They began by attempting to swear him in; something about perjury. He smiled. If only they knew. Sworn in? No. He went straight into his speech.

Hi, my name is Orazio Rige,

Here I stand at an IRS office being asked to account for my actions by a group of men and women who have never accounted for themselves or the sins of their organization. Do you see the hypocrisy? IRS, you're just people. You're not qualified to interrogate me. You're drunk with power because you think you're going to get away with something dastardly because of the immunity of bureaucracy. I assure you, you are not. Those days are over here. **We are the bold.**

I grew up in America. I knew what it meant. I worked hard and prospered. Hurray for me. Now I see an America that I do not recognize. I see hypocrisy and mendacity. I see a regressive society, not a progressive society. That is not acceptable.

There are two kinds of people it seems, givers and takers, builders and destroyers, the sincere and the devious. We can no longer tolerate the takers, destroyers and the devious. We, the givers, the builders and the sincere have been too kind for too long. We have been taken advantage of by people like you. We are no longer the submissive. **We are the Bold.**

Too many times visionaries have been stifled by the fear of the powerful. Sketchy characters who know that their strangleholds are tenuous, and who must protect their metaphorical sandcastle by surrounding them with the dead hopes, dead dreams and even dead bodies of those they fear. We will no longer sacrifice ourselves without a fight. I am a man just as you are a man and as such, we are even. You have had authority in the past, but your irresponsible behavior has disqualified you from any sanctity that your office once enjoyed. In other words, you've done so many things wrong for so long that you no longer have credibility. You're fired, and I will make sure that my authority to do this is respected.

You don't believe me at this moment, but you will.

We are the Bold. We will proceed from here to build things for the betterment of mankind. Medical science, space science and societal reform will move forward at heretofore unseen speed. How is this possible? We will not have our efforts trivialized while our nation's resources are marshalled to achieve voter manipulation. We will not be unencumbered by Salem or Washington D.C. You've become silly. We don't need your permission, and we certainly don't need your obstruction.

The first step in this charge for freedom will be disregard for the court system. It has failed, and its authority is so irrelevant now that regard for it is impossible. The court's rulings are only respected because of police enforcement. The court will find that this cooperation no longer exists. There is not a cop in Oregon who will arrest me. Every one of them knows me, knows who I am, what I do, and that I am not a criminal. So, if you want to send someone after me, do not look to the police. They know that I'm better for Oregon than you. They know it

144

enough to know that you would only act against me with sinister ulterior motives. They know that if you fire them, I'll hire them, and give them a better deal; a deal with dignity.

Throughout history, great men have been decried by authority. For the last five years, I have witnessed genius. Men and women who have made advances in science that authority would never endorse.

- A monetary system that is based on productivity not debt
- A battery that will revolutionize the distribution of energy
- A power plant that has an inexhaustible supply of fuel
- An automobile that is far more economical and romantic than any in existence
- Free distillation of water to build a forest in a desert
- A medical solution to cancer
- A political system that truly represents all of our people
- And so much more

I have also witnessed obstruction. My property was stolen by political thugs. Now, they have enlisted you to come after me. This paper-pusher attack has no substance. My work does. The government that you represent has no power even to protect itself. I do have the power to protect myself. You may not think so at the moment, but you will see. We can do more than you, because we have real skills. You do not. We can build. You can only destroy. You are the desperate. **We are the Bold**.

The courage of one person has always preceded bold steps. Whether it was Madame Curie, Galileo Galilei or Jesus Christ, someone had to stand up and move forward despite the common fear. I am blessed to be among a group of such people. We are not afraid of you. You have no power over us. **We are the Bold**.

Those among us do what we do because we can. We are compelled by our very human nature to build and create. We do not do this to dominate you. In fact, you will be the beneficiary of what we do, and you will get it sooner if you will just get the hell out of our way. You, on the other hand, take great pleasure in dominating us, though you offer nothing. We do not need to defeat you. We simple need to disregard you. You offer nothing. You are nothing but a nuisance.

Each person is an individual. Each person is a minority of one. Don't victimize minorities. There is no telling what one mind can achieve, and we are creatures of mind. Our mind is our gift. We do not have an animal ability to survive through our muscle, fangs and fur. We must use our mind, and use our mind, we most certainly have. Those among us, who have achieved the most through our thoughts and imagination, are the most human among us. Those who thrive through muscle are the most animalistic. For a judge or government to make an unfair ruling and enforce it with violence or the threat of violence is animalistic.

We are the bold. We will not live in devolving society. I have always feared that I would go to my grave having lived in a society that does not meet my standard. Now, I know that a society that will meet and surpass it is possible, even surrounded by animals like you. **We are the Bold**. We will protect ourselves from you. Now, we know we can.

If you are virtuous, and come to my door again with plans to build, you will be embraced. If you come with plans to destroy, as you have today, you will be disempowered. We do not have time and resources for those who waste. We are simply too busy to indulge your witless dependency. We are creators. **We are the Bold.**

We are leaving this room now, we do not threaten retribution for the insulting attempt you have made here today, but if you persist, we will protect ourselves with little regard for the consequences to you. If you pursue us, you bring consequences upon yourself. Remember that. Not all of us are as patient and as kind as I.

I am not sorry you will lose your job over this encounter. This is a terrible job that we will be phasing out soon anyway. You will simply be the first. As the nation watches this live stream, they may wish to interview you. Please remember just how serious we are. Don't forget. We are nothing like what you've ever had to deal with before. We do not tolerate bureaucratic interference. We are always fair. You must be fair and honest too. You thought you were going to hurt me today didn't you? You were okay with that weren't you? We hold you in contempt. You don't have the courage to admit your intention, but in your heart, you know who and what you are. You and your kind are parasites. Now, you have to admit it to yourself. That confession will facilitate a rebirth if you let it. You can be one of us instead of what you once were.

Goodbye, Buddy.

And thank you America for watching and listening. It is a great day for the creators among us.

*****

The IRS agent went back to his desk, only to find that he had been fired. He was instructed to gather his things and leave the building. In shock, he went to his cell phone to call his wife. All that was there was the speech that had just been given to him, playing over and over again.

His car radio was the same. The speech was playing on every station. When he arrived home, his wife was waiting at the door. She asked him what had happened. He said, "Armageddon."

The message played across the country. Orazio knew that he would be supported by many. How many? That depended on the propaganda that The Ten was blowing out.

*****

Rainforest was watching The Ten doing their thing. They knew the plan and were proud that Orazio had told them about the plan without telling The Ten about Rainforest. Rainforest was working with Rige. The Ten was working above Rige. Orazio still wasn't comfortable with the lack of control that The Ten were capable of holding over him, but there wasn't a damn thing he could do about it. He knew someday soon that Rainforest would also rise to regard him as a plebian, but there wasn't anything he could do about that either. These computer people really did have an almost supernatural force at their disposal. They had power to control even the military as displayed by the North Korean missile launching. Ultimately, everybody could be fed disinformation that would control their actions. It was spooky. Orazio Rige couldn't deal with it. It was always going to be over his head. The only way to be in that game was to commit your life to that game and frankly, he just didn't have the aptitude. It worried him at a primal level, but he made enough peace with it to continue.

As the party at Rainforest simmered down, they noticed a guest arriving. It was Lana driving a van? They were each calmly "turned on." Scott, Jimmy and Johnny ran down the stairs to greet the sexy Lana. She was at the door with a big smile on her face that was welcoming but sly.

Lana: How ya doing boys?

The guys were a little tongue-tied.

Scott: Hi Lana, c'mon in. What's with the truck?

Lana: Oh, I have presents for you. I have a proposal for you. A little product research I want you to do for me. You'd be willing to do me a favor wouldn't you?

Scott: I know when I'm being worked, but somehow right now, I'm good with it. What's it you have in mind.

Lana: I have three state-of-the-art sex robots in the truck, and I want you to take them upstairs and live with them for a week or two.

Jimmy: Oh, I'm in. I always wanted to try one of those. They're not Chinese are they? I don't want Chinese AI in my bedroom.

Lana: No, a friend of mine makes these in California.

Scott: Jimmy, you're going to do this?

Jimmy: Hell yeah. Don't you want to try it? It's a tech toy; the ultimate video game. I'm all over it, to coin a phrase.

Scott: What about you Johnny?

Johnny: Well, let's unload them and see if one trips my trigger. You have to be at least curious. I mean, we've looked at them online for like the last ten years. Let's take one out of the box and ….. wow, yeah, I am interested.

Scott: It's true Lana that both of these guys are more adventurous than I. I just feel like I want to save myself for a real woman.

Lana: Scott, this has absolutely nothing to do with women. I will grant you that if you do have a woman, it might be a little dicey trying to get her to accept that this thing is just an appliance, but right now, you don't have that conflict do you?

Scott: Lana, it's not real.

Lana: Dude, it's not a substitute for a person. It's …. Do you jerk off?

Scott: Sometime.

Lana: Is your hand, or your sponge, or your pillow, or whatever you do it with give you this kind of angst?

Scott: No, because I don't make the connection with my hand and an actual woman.

Lana: You use your imagination though don't you? You imagine a woman don't you? I'll bet you imagined me, didn't you? Tell the truth. You'd like to bend me over wouldn't you? You'd like to stick ….

Scott: Stop! I get it, but still.

Lana: Okay Scott, I'll make a deal with you. I'll give you a choice. I'm a one hundred and twenty pound mass of protoplasm. The doll is a sixty pound mass of silicone. You can have me, or the toy. The toy is there for you 24/7 and can be turned off with no hard feelings. I will give you smokin' hot sex a few times a week but you will have to meet the needs of my foibles.

Scott: I was saving myself for a woman, but not necessarily you.

Lana: You're turning me down. Do you realize how mad these other two guys are going to be if you don't screw my guts out at least a few times. You've all wanted to do it. Go for it. I dare you. Or, take one of these Artificial Intelligence toys, have some experience with it, and tell me what you think. I want to invest. I need intelligent objective research. C'mon Scott, don't let the boys go down alone. You'll be the odd man out. I need you the most. These dogs apparently don't have your sensitivity, no offense guys.

Johnny and Jimmy: None taken.

Lana: I'm warning you Scott, if you don't do this for me, I'm going to take you upstairs and sit on your cock until you die. You don't want to risk death do you? Your whole reputation as a man is on the line here.

Scott: Alright, I'll take the fuckin' thing. You know, the potential for double entendre sex jokes with these things seems unavoidable.

Lana: You won't be sorry. When you wake up with a hard on, and you find that squeezy little thing right next to you, and you take a few minutes and think about me and drive it real hard, you'll be glad you did. Then you're free. If you had me there, Oh my God the bullshit you'd have to go through. You'd be tired of me on day three, I guarantee it. The AI girl is a much better deal, at least that's what I think. So yeah, give

151

it a test drive. Orazio Rige's always trying to transform society. I'll bet this does it for a lot of lonely people. I wanna see. I already have one and I love it. I think you will too. And if you ever have a lady walk into your life, drop the thing of at my house for the duration. One way or the other, I'm hoping you'll have all the happiness in the world. And for sure, this is totally just between us, so cheers boys.

Scott: Do you think we should get one for Sammy?

Lana: Sammy? Give that guy a year or two and he'll probably make his own programmable organic woman. That's why I, if you notice, I never let him swab me.

So I'm getting out of here and you dudes can get it on, or uh, get back to what you were doing I mean. Help yourself to unloading the truck. I had to load it all by myself.

The three men unloaded the truck and Lana gave each one of them a kiss on the check and a little squeeze to motivate them to get the assembly started. Driving away she thought, that's Rige, Koz and those three, now we work on the Blacks.

Chapter Sixteen

Oregonism

The speech before the IRS was streamed to all America for six hours, over and over before The Axis shut it down. It had been downloaded more times than anything else in history. It would never stop. The Ten celebrated. They celebrated the success of their dominance of the internet, but even more, they celebrated the success of The Axis taking the bait.

Paradigms are hard to break. The Axis didn't need to be hired and paid. Money has free for the taking with the vulnerabilities of the internet, but somehow The Axis just got a thrill out of taking it from a corrupt government agency. Collusion with destroyers was part of their sociopathy. It was what would ultimately bring them down. The Ten really regarded them as evil children. The Axis existence was very *Lord of the Flies*. The ten regarded themselves as dealing with them as in the last seen of that novel, when the adults finally arrive on the island, and the children take a look at themselves, ashamed at how animalistic they had become.

The success of Rige's business model had not gone unnoticed by the government and by the nation. Being that the genesis of his philosophical transformation of society was Oregon, people had become to affectionately call him *"The Coosneesh"* as a joke moniker remembering *"The Rajneesh."* In fact, the people who were trying to get to Oregon and find a place there called his system **Oregonism**. What they found was that unlike the rest of the country, you couldn't just move there. You needed a job, or a sponsor. There was no "social services" that you could suck off of until you found your place. If you wanted to live the life of Oregonism, you were better off just creating it right where you lived. Oregon was no longer the frontier.

Northern California had already been accepting of the "Contract" style of campaigning. Candidates who wouldn't work within that style were disregarded by voters. They were not yet ready for "Buy Your Votes," but they were starting to drain their Swamps. The Northeast was another story. They saw the wisdom of Buy Your Votes and were starting to propose State Constitutional changes to make it a reality. The economy of Oregon had not only become balanced, the State was operating "in the black." Matty and the Black sisters had influenced all of Oregon's politicians to either openly embrace Rige's Constitution, or do it surreptitiously. The Republican and Democrat Parties in that State simply ceased to exist. Instead, they were replaced by a Union of Voters based on common sense. Merit based government was born.

The government was being run like a profitable business, not with the slavery of a debt based system of control. The whole nation was buying the Helium Batteries, even though there had been no government certification of their safety or even a warranty. The batteries just worked and everybody knew, and everybody wanted them. There was never an advertising campaign for the batteries. The Oregon factory could not keep up with the demand.

The same was true for the Toad. Rod Rodriguez always made sure that priority for the batteries was his brother's car business, so Oscar knew that he never had to worry about his supply of America's hottest commodity. Oregon was flush with cash, and flush with tax free bartering. It was an economic boom greater than any gold rush. The quality of life there was escalating quickly and every person knew the thanks went to Orazio Rige and his idealistic friends.

The manufacture and selling of the Toad hadn't gone outside the Rige Coos Bay company yet, but Oscar and his family were making them as fast as they could, and each one was presold, so each one of these personally crafted vehicles would ultimately be a collector's item. There were autographs on the cars, and even color mix formulas for the custom color each car sported at the buyer's request.

Orazio was working with Oscar and a manufacturing consultant from Washington State to set up the Toad's mass production factory. Oscar wanted to keep his place as a custom shop, and let a big commercial factory make the generic ones for mass distribution. He was proud that each one he made for the presold clientele was unique. He wanted his original shop to remain special. Specialty personal car builders were really who he and his family were. The money from the big business would be appreciated and earned, but just not the life dream of the show-car wizards.

Speaking of cash, the X was also being adopted everywhere. People just used it. The government couldn't stop it. Battery purchases with the X were lower than the cost of purchases with America's deflating cash. The demand for new cash in America went to zero. Suddenly, there was no need for a Federal Reserve. It wasn't ready to be disbanded yet, but it soon would. Wealth was being made for trade, instead of cash being borrowed from God knows who. The X was backed by the full faith and credit of manufacturing, not military control.

The military was not hurt by this. Orazio Rige made it clear to them that he intended for them to protect the planet's tyrants from the invincible high-ground of space, and the nation's funding of America's newly conceived "Space Force" was a top priority. Ground fighting would become pointless. No troops would ever be in danger again. International policing problems could be addressed from instantly strategic platforms in Earth orbit. Bad actors could be eliminated with robotic drone attacks, personalized with facial recognition programs. Drones never sleep. Old style tyrants could never rise to power. They would be "nipped in the bud." Therefore, funding of the military would not be diminished, simply directed toward more high-tech systems. The military would evolve to be efficiently "Oregonized." Also, since the military directives were simple in their singularly encompassing nature, there would be no real need for constant lobbying. Military money would be spent as expeditiously as the self-sanitizing system would allow. You can't steal something that's already gifted to you.

Washington State was the local hold out. They erected a virtual "Iron Curtain" at their border with Oregon. The State's number one industry is government. The metaphorical tide was rising on the metaphorical sandcastles there. There were many aspects of the Rige Constitution that were hard for special interest groups to take. In Washington, a huge one was the family law industry. Washington State was taking obscene Federal funding for child support and spousal support enforcement. This seemed surprising to Orazio because he'd thought a politically correct society wouldn't insult women by considering them to be too dependent to fend for themselves, but they do. He was unaware of the Federal funding scam for this purpose, and how local jurisdictions abused it. Few are aware of this scam. Orazio knew he would have to expose it and stop it. It seemed that in Washington, hypocrisy of failure to observe equal protection just hasn't been recognized. The truth was, the Federal funds supported an immeasurable bureaucracy of women who went to college, but failed to take productive education courses. What are you going to do with a Women's Studies degree? Victimize men! It's bullshit.

The State economy had nothing to fear in its status as a major harbor in Puget Sound. That was productivity based wealth. The real reason for Washington's resistance was brain drain. Washington has the highest concentration of STEM kids in the country. These kids were beginning to figure out that they had the power to control the State, and the entrenched dinosaurs of politics there were not yet ready to concede to evolution, not without a fight.

In a realization that would have made Martin Luther proud, the STEM kids of Washington State began to understand that their skills were more powerful than an inept, bloated government bureaucracy. They knew they could break from their existing power structure, just as Martin Luther had in breaking from the Catholic Church. They politely called their underground movement, *Our Reformation*. Behind closed doors it was often referred to as *The Tech Mafia*. They already had their people in government, why not control it?

The social media propaganda companies were hired to use their considerable resources to demonize Oregonism. The Ten reveled in this action; more government colluding with The Axis. How much of Washington's computer talent would spiral into the quicksand of a failing government? The shakeup would destroy Washington's bureaucracy from within. Especially from those who have been abused by family court. It was literally a sit back and watch situation. The techs who found the environment not conducive to their success would begin to look for a better place to play. Washington would be on the wrong side of history and make the wrong bet, especially as the government currency continued to devalue.

Rige turned his back on Washington, knowing that he would get their STEM kids minds by the merit of the freedom he offered them. He turned his sights to California. He didn't want to buy the State and move the border. He had entertained the idea, but felt it crossed a line of ethics. Rainforest came up with the idea. Just divide the State.

California was not like Oregon. When Rige started his onslaught, no one knew. It started quietly, and grew unnoticed until it was too big to stop. Now, the cat was out of the bag. The whole country was watching. California had an economy greater than most countries. It was controlled by crime families in conjunction with labor unions, and fortified by legions of useful idiots in media and education. It was too big and had too many sectors of special interests for Rige to buy his way to victory. It would have to be done with philosophy. *New California* became the name for that resistance movement.

The size of California and its formidable economy that made it strong was also its Achilles Heel. It was unmanageable because of its lack of centralization. Too many cultures, too many ethnicities, too many sub-economies made the State vulnerable to division. In union there is strength. In diversity is eventual fragmentation. The crime families of California were "outed" by propaganda from The Ten. Union control was also exposed. The vast majority of people in the State realized that in the "Us and Them" of their State, they were the "Them." The resentment created "*New California.*" The divided State was real. It only had to be somehow put on paper. Old California held its ground, but New California with its larger population and larger land area did too.

New Hampshire didn't have that problem. It was a manageable size. New Hampshire was the first State to totally adopt Oregonism and its Constitution. They fully adopted "Buy Your Votes" as part of it. They were using both currencies because the X was nowhere near in general use. It was still a boutique monetary system, and compared to the weight of the United States economy, it would be for years to come. There was no getting around that, but the undeniable fact was, the X had no debt attached to it. The X would eventually prevail, or at least another monetary system like it would. Either way, the Federal Reserve would be recognized for its crimes and eventually just abandoned; abandoned without regard for the fiat debt it held over the poor stupid Americans who had allowed it for over one hundred years.

New Hampshire's economy immediately began to swell. The real estate there doubled in value overnight. People, especially divorced men, began to migrate there. The idea of a court system that was forced to be fair was all they were looking for. They would work for peanuts if only they were allowed to keep the peanuts. In Oregon and New Hampshire, they could. Despite their willingness to be submissive to a kinder master, they found that they weren't exploited. Those FORGOTTEN MEN were appreciated for their skills, and their past was of no consequence. In fact, it was never known. Suddenly, recognition of the wisdom of Oregonism hit everybody. Within two years the entire Northeast adopted the new political structure.

In one election cycle, whole areas of government programs were dissolved. The northeast became a bastion of

"Give us your Best, and you'll get more than you ever dreamed." It became not an option, but the only path. People who couldn't understand this had to flee to Southern States that were running the old scam of welfare for control. People in the Northeast who were truly in need of public support for medical problems or disability found that the growing economies there, plus the loss of a "welfare queen" or illegal alien population provided incredibly compassionate accommodations from both the hospitals and the churches. The good in people toward their fellow man was found to be generously voluntary. All you had to do in any such community was point to a need, and it would be immediately addressed. That was the nature of the prosperous society. Compassion flowed from the heart, not from compulsion. Help for our needy became personal and based on love, with the whole community involved. The philosophical transformation was beautiful. You didn't have some cold government program based on rationed rights. You had the warmth of belonging to a family that would never let you down, and even invite you to grow with it.

*****

All during the political upheaval of politics in America, other aspects of life were being reinvented. Tidal pumps were forcing ocean water up the mountains to lakes that were higher in elevation than Dana Morea's forest. This wasn't the irrigation water from the steam generated by the power plants. This was simple ocean water pumped to chasms in mountain desert areas above the timberline. There, the water would be purified as it made its way down through the rock of the mountain's structure, eventually into the water table.

The real purpose for the lakes was an engineering idea that Dana had for years. The lake would provide water pressure for the land below. Dana loved her forest and wanted to fire proof it. The plan was simple. Using the irrigation piping, the distilled irrigation water could be turned off, and the ocean lake water could be turned on in sectors. Surrounding the forest was a perimeter of perforated pipe that would launch the ocean water, pressurized naturally by gravity, about thirty feet into the air. You wouldn't even need a pump. The forest was surrounded so fire would have a hard time entering. If fire did breach the perimeter, sectors within the forest could have their fire prevention water turned on. The fire would be put down quickly and efficiently. No endangering firefighters, no loss of control, and most of all, virtually no cost.

Most people in the world live either on the coast or in valleys. Dana felt that new buildings under construction should be built with roof top sprinklers. Fire in a city would be easily put down. If a building went on fire, you would turn on its firefighting sprinklers, and you would turn on the sprinklers of the buildings next door. Buildings already have pipes all throughout. Why not have pipes across the perimeter of the roof with heads about every twenty feet apart? Isn't this idea obvious? In places like California where there are always seasonal forest fires, why not have perforated pipe across the top of every mountain ridge? Fire sweeps up a mountain, but runs down slowly. When a fire is discovered, wouldn't it be great to simply turn on strategic sprinkler pipes to isolate the fire when it is first found? California is next to the Pacific Ocean and has a mountain range across its entire length. Why hasn't this been done? Dana just couldn't imagine. She protected her beloved forest, and hoped everybody else would love and protect theirs.

*****

The other big change taking place was the nature of millennial men. Orazio wasn't sure why it was, but his observation was that millennial men were not like him. As a young man he was always on the prowl for a sexy girl. Even though he worked hard to build his business, it was always foremost in his mind to share it with the woman of his heart's desire. The respect of men was easy. If you were successful in business and reasonable affable, guys would like you. What Orazio Rige wanted was to be admired by women. He wanted to fall in love with a woman that he admired. His success wouldn't and couldn't be complete without it. He thought this was the nature of all men, and equally, the natural, complementary desire of any good woman.

His observation of millennial men showed something very different. Young men seemed to regard women as a source of problems as opposed to a source of completion of the half of the organism that was them together. Orazio Rige felt that a man needed a woman and a woman needed a man to be whole. Young millennial men seemed self-satisfied, or not even satisfied, self-neglected. Where Orazio felt that a man needed to serve a woman and that woman needed to be equally committed to serving her man, the millennials seemed not only to avoid, but to be avoided by women. Orazio felt that nature was being violated and the violation would end in doom.

He asked Carole for her thoughts and she was equally absent of perspective. In attempting to empathize with one young man for his apparent depression or nihilism, he showed no interest in reparation. He said, "If there's something wrong with me, go ahead and cure it, in the meantime, I'm fine." He was beyond apathy. He didn't recognize that his condition was not normal and therefore didn't see a reason to address it. He didn't see a reason to live, and didn't see a reason not to. Was he okay? Neither Carole nor Orazio could relate.

Their suspicion was lack of fathers in the lives of young men, radical feminism, unfair education systems from kindergarten to college, unfair workplace practices, the Title IX legal mess, prejudicial courts, bad divorce rulings, prejudicial hiring practices, geeez, now I'm depressed; maybe even bad diet. They could see one thing clearly from Lana and her sex robot business. The machines were selling. Young men had no use for a society that considered them criminals for their very existence, so they opted out. The robots were a wonderful surrogate. The funniest part of the whole robot friend phenomenon was that the guys treated their companions like a queen. Men are capable of great love. Many love a guitar, a fishing rig. a rifle, a motorcycle, a car, a computer and a team member, a chess playing partner or golf partner, or even a personal skill like doing fine surgery, or just an excellent tattoo.

The personal companion was a perfectly good object of affection, and the best part of it was, it would never betray you. Most men who lived with such a robot were inexplicably happy. They could indulge their nature and venture out to conquer, knowing that they had a warm and happy home to come home to.

Millennial women were not happy. Women by nature are nesters, not generally audacious or daring. They may flirt with the idea of venturing out, some can for a while, but generally, their nature is to stay home and send their man out to bring home the spoils of his pluck. Bring it home to them.

Now they sat home alone. No man was coming home to them, and why? They had pushed their empowerment too far. You are not entitled to a man. The power of women is to have a man by satisfying that man, not mastering him. If there is no love waiting for a man in your arms, you will soon find your arms empty. This was what society had wrought; a world hostile to men; a world so hostile that men used their incredible ingenuity to repair it in their own way. The proof in the pudding is in the eating, and the truth was, the artificial intelligence companions were so satisfying, that the thought of the complexity and danger of dealing with a societally indoctrinated woman was lost.

The robots were never a problem. A relationship with a woman would be fraught with dissatisfaction. Then there was the financial aspect. The cost and maintenance of the robot was a huge savings. Nobody, was saying a robot was a substitute for a woman, but so many men all pretty much agreed that despite your commitment to not being able to have both, the robot was the unquestionably better deal.

Orazio just didn't get it, but millions of men and even some hopelessly resigned women did. Lana was making a fortune. Her company, headquartered in Oregon, was called *Oregasm*.

Chapter Seventeen

Federal Metamorphosis

The Federal Government was fighting back. As people all over the country began to create products and services, and market them without government license, the Federal government fell back on the old scare tactics. The government put out a propaganda campaign stressing the need for safety that could only be provided by its safety-crats such as the Food and Drug Administration (the FDA). They cried, how can you trust an unlicensed doctor or lawyer? How can you be sure your food and your drugs are safe without government oversight? What about vehicles and school curriculum? The court system joined in. If you want a ruling in court, you must be represented by a licensed lawyer.

Why? The law should be simple. If the law is so complicated that there is too much ambiguity, the law needs to be simplified and presented in simple language. Legalese is bullshit. Legalese is a way to make law inaccessible to the common man. The unnecessary complexity needs repair. If the court system is so complicated that you need a professional to navigate it, that system needs to be brought back to reality as well. Why would you use a system that insults you? People simply began to disregard the pompous court, and the financial cost it incurs when you try to work with it.

It was too late for the government to stop independent technicians and entrepreneurs. People were already used to their own system of control. They had used it for years with companies like Amazon and Uber. It was simple; the market had a rating system for everything. If you didn't deliver on your promises, you'd get bad reviews, you'd be out of business. If you hurt someone, it would be immediately known. Retribution would follow. The social media was so strong when it came to dissatisfaction getting out that no scam could last very long, and scammers would be scammers whether there was government control or not, so the government involvement was moot.

The people had lifetimes of bad doctors, bad lawyers, bad clergy, bad teachers, bad judges, bad cops, bad investment advisors, and bad bureaucrats. The government had lost credibility with the people in general. The government was beginning to be viewed as not your protector, but in reality, just a robber really. The idea that they were not providing a valuable service was realized. People were working around the government and its cost in money and obstruction.

The issue really came to a head when the work of Sammy Zane escaped the secrecy it had worked under for the previous three years. Too many people in the Rige Coos Bay Company had been cured of too many medical maladies to hide it any longer. Doctor Zane had hopeful volunteers who took radical treatments on a gamble and were cured of their inoperable conditions. One way he did this was through gene manipulation. He would isolate the damaged gene that was allowing the malignant cells to grow, and replaced them with undamaged DNA strands from any donor organism. Since all DNA shares the same chemical structure, and the only difference is in their nucleotide sequence, any healthy DNA is useful DNA. The other method was to remove the damaged DNA and replace it with cloned DNA. Since the DNA chain is a double helix, (like a ladder) there are two sides, a healthy side and a damaged side. Somewhere along the chain, you simply clone the good side. The practice isn't easy, but the idea is. Doctor Zane's had mastered the practice.

The epigenetic field exploded with doctors who were already competent, but simply held back by the FDA. The people wanted their medical miracles. Their resentment for government bureaucracy grew personal and immediate for millions of people. They wanted the damned government with its pharmaceutical company profiteers out of the way.

*****

State governments begin to realize that the role of the Federal Government must be restricted to simply as stated in the original concept of the Founding Fathers. Each State, by both the government and the private sector, easily saw where all they needed from the Federal Government was for them to deal with international issues. Federal departments of education, employment, health and welfare are not consistent with the needs of anybody. Each State asserted its sovereignty. Money sent to the Federal government came under extreme scrutiny. People wanted accountability. Basically, they wanted to get what they paid for. The Federal budget was slashed. Money for the military stayed the same, but Social Security and Medicare would have to be relegated to the States, who through the productivity of Oregonism were well able to take care of their own people in a smaller, more controlled environment. Corruption and graft became much more difficult.

America left the United Nations because the whole world was beginning to see the wisdom of Oregonism, and therefore the motivation for war, based on economics, became untenable. Religious war also was demilitarized by the Space Force. Peace was maintained by monitoring military buildup and stopping it. Pray to whoever you like, but "If you want what we have, make it yourself. We'll show you how. Don't come here to take ours. We'll kill you if you try," became the international law. This law was not enforced by a nation. It was basically enforced by The Ten. Remember, The Ten had real power. They had the power of capability. They could make things happen. Bureaucrats had no real power, and their former power through corruption was being recognized and was being dismantled.

At this point, Oregonism was adopted in some form by all fifty States. Buy Your Vote was the hard part. The paradigms of the past were so entrenched in even the electorate that a great deal of education was necessary to get people to understand how it worked. Each State rewrote the State Constitution that Orazio Rige had written for Oregon. It amazed Orazio how people held onto their prejudices. People fought for things like sanctuary State status, even though the idea was a proven liability. "Don't come here. Make your own damn country work," was the wisdom of Oregonism. The indoctrination of the former education system had left its damage that would take a generation to cleanse. Some brain-washing leaves a stain that can never be cleaned up. Doubt is a terrible thing, and having years of training in believing that you and your country are bad leaves that immutable doubt, always in the back of your mind. A lot of people were permanently psychologically damaged this way. The brain-washing was started at such a young age and carried through their entire educational life that it was immutably ingrained.

California provided a shocking display of commitment to its new Constitution. It reconstituted from a divided State as New California. The movement had won, and kept its banner intact. California was transformed from an Oligarchy, to a State run by its vast diversity of capable people. It was significant because it sent a message to the Federal

Government. "As goes California, so goes the nation." The Federal Government was not going down without a fight. The Axis was hired to attack Oregonism and was licensed to kill.

The bloodshed began. Where The Ten and The Axis had always fought a cyber battle, now, they were sending out the jackals to kill The Ten physically. It was hot-war. The Ten responded in kind. It became a violent manhunt, the ultimate in stalking. Resources beyond the imagination of the common man came into play. Nobody was safe from the intrusion into the lives of every American. Everybody was watched. Incredibly complex algorithms based on wild paranoia were conceived and written to hunt down anybody who might be useful in flushing out the prey of The Axis and The Ten, by The Axis and The Ten. Parents, children, friends and lovers, anybody even remotely connected to anyone suspected of being involved in any way with The Ten was stalked.

The Axis had an advantage. Their sociopathy allowed them to kill everybody if necessary. They had no one to protect because they had no synergy with the rest of society. They considered themselves to be masters. To them, everybody was expendable.

Conversely, The Ten was compelled to protect everybody, but any protection rendered would tip off The Axis as to the value of the protected. It was an exercise in international intrigue like none before. People were disappearing without anyone knowing if it was for their protection, or if they were dead. At the same time, The Ten had to be ruthless in its protection of people. You had to kill the killers because there was no police force to work with, and the killers would never stop, and worked far outside any law.

Everything was secret until suddenly, the bullets, poisons, knives or garrotes finished a job, and a person.

The greatest fear of The Ten had come to pass. They had always known of the possibility of this kind of move from the cyber world to the corporal world, and thought they were ready in many ways. The brutality of the whole thing, and the psychological damage to them was more real and immediate than any of them could have imagined. Because of their man Bobby Diez, the entire Toad Company had to disappear. The idea of those families becoming hostages was more than Orazio Rige could stand. Hiding that many people was just crazy. Moving them to a different country wouldn't help at all. The Axis was so international that it didn't even consider borders. The team that was able to take on the task was The Black sisters and Lana. The three of them had friends in low places. Lana was a desert fighter by trade, and Marla and Donna Black were very clever at hiding things in an "analog" way. The ladies had done a lot of work that was "all cash." They moved everybody associated with Toad to a valley in Nevada that had been originally bought by Dana Morea under a corporate name. The trick was to provide all those people with food without attracting attention. They managed to pull off the camping trip for the two months of savagery.

The computer world moves fast. The leaders of both The Ten and The Axis were flushed out by each other and killed. The computer world also knows the value of redundancy, so there were a few people to keep both organizations working for a few more days, but they too were quickly located and terminated. Without their heads, both organizations were dead. Operatives down the line of succession had no reason to continue. The government's power that had been sought by hiring The Axis in the first place had no one to turn to, to continue. The Federal Government had to concede defeat. It was now under the control of the State Governments who provided its finances. It now had to do its job under the American Constitution. It no longer had the ability to usurp power. The U.S. Constitution would have to be followed to the letter. The Supreme Court would also have to adhere to strict enforcement if it even wanted to survive at all. No more politics from the bench. Politics had changed too much for that now. There was too much citizen oversight for wild corruption. The new rules were, "obey the rules."

With the Federal Government under control, the Federal Reserve had no more use. The House of Representatives wrote and passed legislation to revoke The Federal Reserve Act which licensed the organization to control America's money supply. With the Federal Reserve removed, there was no need to regard the principle and interest that the bank had imposed on America during its time in operation. It was simply closed with the resolution of the American people to never allow slavery of debt to be institutionalized in America ever again. The officers of the Federal Reserve were allowed to walk away with no fear of prosecution for their crimes. The States simply wanted to turn our back on a savage period in our nation's history and move on with slavery finally abolished.

The huge problem left by the cyber-human war was that the control of the military that The Ten had integrated into worldwide humanitarian policing was gone. Not only did The Ten and The Axis kill each other, they also killed their computers. Both companies did the obvious for people of their perception of value. Both built viruses to infect each other's computers rendering them irreparably useless. In their arrogance, The Ten's computers were linked enough to military computer systems that the viruses took out the military computer systems. They all had to be wiped, and I don't mean "wiped with a cloth." The company known as Main would have been the natural successor, but during the cyber-human war, they disbanded. They didn't have the stomach to see themselves drawn in. The entire military had to be rebooted, and the only one left to do it was Rainforest. Rainforest had remained unknown enough to prepare for the day when they were the last man standing, and that day had arrived. Other countries were making every attempt to infiltrate the American military remnants, but their computers became infected with the Cyber-human war viruses too. Rainforest had remained untainted.

The aftermath of every war empowers any world power that hasn't been destroyed by it. Somebody somewhere still has some money to buy the rest of the devastated world at discount prices. Rainforest and Rige Coos Bay were ready. Rige Coos Bay had been protected by Rainforest's firewalls throughout the bloodbath. It not only protected the core company, but all of the branch corporations. Toad Motors, Helium Battery, Geothermal Power, X Exchange, and even Brother's Space Enterprise was secure. That protection had been Rainforest's primary task as dictated by Rige and fully acknowledged by Rainforest. The foresight and gamesmanship of their plan was winning the day. Not only the critical systems of the military were compromised, but the rest of the Federal Government had been locked in to The Axis as part of their plan for world domination. Rainforest would have to reboot the Federal Government as well. This reboot would allow Rainforest to make sweeping changes to the government. All previous records had been destroyed. The government could be restarted clean.

Chapter Eighteen

Ratzi and Carole

Brother's Space Enterprise was experimenting with full size robotic ships. They were successfully launching their vehicles into space and returning them safely to the Earth. Since it was all done with magnetism, there was very little drama in the usual space program sense. Since human life was not at risk in the experiments, there was a safety factor that was undeniable. The only safety issue would have come from vehicles slipping out of the magnetic envelope that propelled them through an electrical power failure. Brother's had plenty of power backup sources. Batteries couldn't be the source, so capacitive discharge was the obvious choice for the short but intense power demand it would take to prevent a disaster. Murray Atkins had thought of everything and was in full control of his visionary hardware.

He decided to attempt a bold experiment in space mining. He wanted to launch a vehicle into space with the goal of capturing an asteroid and bringing it back to Earth. He approached Orazio Rige for the money it would take to build something that large, and Rige had no trouble in providing it. The Toad had gone national and it was working just as Oscar Rodriguez had imagined. His own factory still couldn't keep up with the demand, and aftermarket businesses were opening all over the country to create custom modifications to each individual's cars. Most people just appreciated the low cost and easy maintenance of the car as ordered, but the aftermarket was so seductive that almost everybody had some custom doodad whether interior or exterior to set themselves apart, even if it was just a custom wrap finish, and God knows, there were plenty of those. The other even bigger income source came from the helium battery. The Black sisters had been very thorough about international intellectual property protection, and Rainforest was there to make sure that protection was enforced. "You want the batteries, you buy them from us." Rige had more money than any childhood dream, wealth "Beyond the Dreams of Avarice."

The mining vehicle was launched and was watched by the world. It captured a rock about half the size of a football field that though weightless in space, on Earth weighed about 20,000 tons. When it was captured it was moving at a relative speed of 38,000 miles per hour. Velocity in space is easy to overcome. All you need is gentile resistance for a long period of time. Aggressive resistance could cause the effect of an impact and deform or even fragment the stone. The mining vehicle slowly and gently dragged the stone to a stop and redirected it into a geosynchronous orbit above the Earth. That was where the hard part started. The stone had to be very slowly descended to Oregon without creating the heat of entry that a meteorite would experience. It also had to be brought down in resistance to the Earth's gravity so that it would land gently as opposed to crashing. It was a big rock, and even without the energy of its 38,000 mph space flight speed, just falling would be a destructive crash.

History was being made in an almost science fiction way. As the rock was slowly descended to the ground, Orazio Rige could hardly believe the accomplishment of amateur physicist Murray Atkins and his young dedicated, visionary team. He wondered what else the minds of people could dream up, pursue and achieve. The gigantic rock was placed on the ground as delicately as you would set down a baby. The mining vehicle on top of it, ascended, hovered and was directed to a spot about a hundred feet away. Its tiny size compared to the stone was shocking. Since it was simply an antenna for the focus of an electromagnetic field, it didn't have to be very big at all. It wasn't a mining car; it was just a field generator. Proportionately, it was like the electric motor in your refrigerator. It was fully ready for inspection, and then with any luck, its next mission.

There it sat; material from space. Murray looked at Dana Morea and said, "Have at it." Dana had her geologist friends assembled and they approached it like Moonwatcher in *2001, a Space Odyssey.* It wasn't even hot. The awesomeness, if that's an actual word, was felt so deeply that it could only be described as reverence. They began their analysis slowly at first, but realized that in reality, it was there to be mined. It was mostly iron and water, which had the shocking characteristic of melting. Without the icy cold of space, the asteroid was melting into the ground. Dana could hardly contain herself. She was ecstatic to see how much water was there. The geologists continued. Right up on the surface there seemed to be a gold vein. As it turned out, there was over a hundred pounds of gold in the thing. Murray had it removed and offered everyone on the team a twelve gram commemorative ring he had designed. He had originally just thought the ring would be any metal, probably iron, but when he saw the gold, he felt that he and the project were blessed. It was so much more than just gold. He felt that the rings were sanctified.

He gave two of the rings to Orazio and Carole Kozlowski of course, and in a gesture he was proud of to his very core, gave Orazio the rest of the gold. The lump of gold when refined turned out to be about the size of three quarters of a gallon. He had an idea about something special to do with

175

some of that gold, something he had wanted to do for a long time.

Carole looked at him and said, "Ratzi, you've gotten everything you imagined and so much more. You're revolutionized government and the economy which was your goal the first night we talked about this. You've empowered visionary inventors to realize their dreams. You've made your mark by helping countless people make theirs. Most fortunate for you, you made friends. You made friends with people who are proud to be your friend. There is no greater measure of success. You wanna take a day off?"

"No Carole," Orazio said. "I don't want to take a day off. There's one thing I want to do more than anything else right now. I want to marry you and have a house full of kids, our kids. Will you marry me?" Carole melted into Orazio's arms. She said, "I have to, I could never say yes to any other man. I love you, and will be by your side forever. I always would have been anyway. Let's go get the first pregnancy started and then we'll call the Homestead."

Orazio said, "At last, I'm not doomed."

*****

The wedding was a reunion of people who had in many cases never met. The Homestead was hired for a week, so there would be time to prepare and time clean up after the event of a lifetime. The event took place over two full days, and for several passed out guests, three days. There were literally shifts of chefs, bar tenders and service staff. The restaurant was open around the clock. People came, went and came back. Every hotel within fifty miles was booked the day after the marriage proposal was made, and even though the wedding was just a month later, Ratzi and Carole had to make emergency accommodations at Rige Coos Bay for the overflow of the massive company's wonderful people. The couple knew they had friends, but seeing them all assembled in one place was too sentimental.

Saturday morning didn't even start slowly. The Black sisters were actually staying in one of the dining rooms that wasn't being used for dining. They were there on Friday, and seemed to never sleep. Ratzi's best man was Sir Ashton Mathews the third, and the Bride was given away by Carole's father who insisted his wife be right there at his side. "Joined at the hip," he said. Carole's sisters were there of course, and her brother who fly in from New York. He had cloistered the family when the war took place. He had a bugout place upstate and the family had a code word. His apocalypse prepper plans had paid off, and he knew Orazio appreciated it.

The place was swamped with appreciative politicians who had risen to their position as a result of Oregonism. Orazio was never the handshaking type so he seemed a little standoffish, but nobody was going to disdain their appreciated shot-caller. The guy he was looking for was Ryan Chang, and there he was with his wife, son and daughter. Handshake, he hugged Ryan. The two of them just smiled at each other, speechless. Ryan held up his right hand to show Ratzi the Brother's Space Enterprise ring. Ryan's wife said, "You don't know what it meant to Ryan that you included him with the Brother's project." Ratzi hugged Ryan again.

Ratzi recognized his brother Vito was talking to Rod Rodriguez and Mitch Roggenbuck. He walked over and Rod said, "Your brother has a good idea. I already thought of it, but it's still a good idea, see ….

177

Ratzi said excuse me. He saw Carole talking to about twenty women dressed in wild cocktail clothes. He suddenly realized, its Carole's friends at Toad. They're here. The parking lot reserved for them has gotta be ..... He went outside and there it was; the car show. Some Toad cars sure, but the real heavy shit was there, beautiful Caddys, and every Chevy, Chevy ever made. There were antique low riders with paint, chrome and interiors done with pure love. The show was machismo and respect all rolled into one. This is who we are, and we're here for you. Ratzi Rige walked right over to Oscar Rodriguez and asked, "Xiomara drive the Chevelle?" Oscar smiled, "You know it *jefe*." Ratzi said, "I saw her inside talking to Carole."

Oscar: She loves her man.

Orazio: I know. Carole loves your whole family, and now, you're going to finally meet ours. My dad is like you, he worked hard to give me everything, and my mom is like yours, nothing too good for her *figlio*, her son.

Oscar: Where they at? Oh, I'm sorry Whiteman boss; I'm supposed to act like a millionaire business man. So pardon me, so, where are they?

Orazio: Oscar, you are definitely my favorite racist. My dad's on the front porch smoking a cigar, and my mom is in the kitchen making him something to eat.

Oscar: I like 'em already.

Orazio: Find me later, I'll introduce you. Right now, I wanna see your cars.

As they walked into the parking lot, Ratzi Rige was surrounded by dozens of guys, their ladies, and what seemed like a hundred kids. The cars were beautiful of course, but even more beautiful were the happy people.

Dana Morea looked more lovely than Ratzi had thought possible. He said, "Dana is that you?" She answered back, "Fuck you, Carole made me do this."

Ratzi: You're beautiful, you look like a girl.

Dana: Yeah, Carole took me for an embarrassing spa day, followed by clothes shopping until I couldn't take it anymore. She has me all hair dressed and coochied up like a *giovane puttana.*

Ratzi: No, that's crazy. You don't look like a little whore, you look tasteful and attractive. You look like the lovely woman that was always in there somewhere. Now go look in the mirror and resign yourself to the fact that you're a little heart-breaker. And don't forget to thank Carole, she loves you. Make that your wedding gift to her, do you hear me bitch?

Dana: Bitch? Ratzi Rige you are my friend. Thank you for accepting me the way I am. I am grateful for Carole's attention. It's more than I deserved.

Ratzi: Not at all Dana, and though it may break your heart to hear me say it, I love you too.

Dana Morea reached over and hugged Orazio. She broke the hug, walked away and didn't look back, and then stopped, and then did.

Orazio couldn't help noticing three guys who were sizing up the crowd. He asked a few of his security people to accompany him as he went over to address them.

Orazio: Hi gentlemen, thank you for coming to my wedding, I'm afraid I'm not the best with faces, do I know you?

The first man: Mr. Rige, we have never met in person, but have always wanted to. My name is Patrick Dryden, this is Jim Cleary, and this gentleman is Hakim Hassan. We were on an oil tanker that you hired which was hijacked. What you did for us and the whole crew of that ship, well, it gave a lot of us better lives, especially Hakim here. We came to meet you and thank you.

Orazio: Well I'm honored to meet you. You were certainly brave and I guess bravery has been called upon by each of you, God, probably too many times.

The second man: Thank you. That recognition is good to hear.

Orazio: I hope you're not insulted that I approached you with security.

The first man: Insulted? We'd be disappointed if you didn't.

Orazio: Hakim was it?

Hakim: Yes sir.

Orazio: Hakim, can I guess you served with these guys in the Middle East somewhere?

Hakim: Actually, we never met until that day on the ship.

Orazio: Listen guys, I really want to hear your whole story. Would you be my guest soon and tell me your memory about what happened that day?

The first man: Of course we will. Can we call your office?

Orazio: I'm going to honeymoon for a week or two and then we'll spend some time together. Do any of you have contact information?

The first man: Do you want to put my number in your phone?

Orazio: Good idea. And now, just so these security guys can stand down, this is my wedding, you don't have to sweep my guests. It's your job today to eat and drink and enjoy life. If you do that and nothing else, it will be your wedding gift to me, okay?

The men all nodded and stood somewhat at attention until Ratzi Rige walked away. He saw them from time to time doing just what he had asked. Even the security guys said they really loosened up. Mr. Rige reflected on his blessings. Those highly trained men were trusting his security to do the thing they were trained to do. That fact made him grateful that he could give them that. Imagine.

There she stood, Lana. Just as Ratzi approached her, Carole returned from God knows where. The three of them stood about four feet apart and just looked back and forth like a Mexican standoff. Finally Lana said, "My work here is done," and the three of them just burst out laughing.

Lana: So Ratzi, I don't suppose I could interest you in an artificial intelligence product?

Carole: No Lana, we're going with organic intelligence.

Lana: Well, it couldn't happen to a better matched couple. You too are going to be obscenely happy. People like you are nothing but a problem for my business, with all your satisfaction and quality time; gives me the shivers.

Ratzi: You know Lana, I never did really believe in the sex doll thing, but I've seen how happy people are with it. I guess I'm just an old fashioned guy.

Lana: Well, you may not believe it coming from me, but I've actually made a clinic for people who want to make the crossover from AI to human. We're looking for a healthy transition for people who want children. We all know that kids need both parents, the studies are conclusive, and so when the yen to reproduce comes about, we want to make sure that people can make that transition without any loss of satisfaction or dignity; its's tricky, but important.

Carole: Wow Lana, that's very altruistic from a pessimist like you.

Lana: Actually Carole, we're finding big money in it.

Carole: You've got to be kidding.

Ratzi: Yes of course she's kidding, right Lana.

Lana looked at them quizzically and said, "Oh, I'll catch up with you both later, there's a guy I want to talk to" and trotted off.

Carole: Ratzi, why did you have security when you were talking with those men?

Ratzi: Oh my God Carole. Those guys, those guys were the ones on the hijacked tanker. They're used to securing their location. They were actually protecting us, until I asked them to stand down and let my people handle it. I'm going to meet with them after our honeymoon and finally hear their story. I would have you with us, but I want to hear it man to man, if you .....

Carole: No, you're right. I'll watch the recording. Let them tell you and only you. It will be better that way.

Ratzi: I love you Carole.

Carole: Ratzi, I always had faith, but there were times I did think we wouldn't get out of this alive.

Ratzi: I know babe, frankly, I was afraid to marry you until now. I was never sure if putting you by my side would make you a target, but now, we're not going to have to upset anymore apple carts. I really think we can just be family. I'm going to delegate all throughout the business and step back. We're going to raise kids, not money.

Carole took Orazio's arm and began to walk back to the restaurant. She knew he was getting hungry. Before they could even get through the door, Murray Atkins with Lucas Vasquez tagging along bumped into them. Lucas was all grown up now, and was a good engineer in his own right. Murray looked at Orazio and Carole, and said, "Congratulations to both of you. You are an incredible couple. Look at your friends. Talk about putting down roots. Man you've got it all, and right here on Earth. I'm so happy for you. When you get a chance in a month or so, I'd like to get together with you for a little recap of the plans for the future. You, on the other hand have your future all laid out in front of you and it looks beautiful." Lucas chimed in with, "Yes congratulations. I can't imagine what it must be like for you. I've never seen a bigger family and you know how my dad and mom are. It's all a lot to take in, congratulations again. Murray's engaged you know. Got an astrophysicist babe form JPL. She came up here and set up her own magnetic field. Murray's doomed." Carole and Ratzi laughed and Carole said, "I can't believe he said doomed. The young man asked, was that rude, I'm sorry. No Carole said, it's just what Ratzi always says, it was just funny hearing it from somebody else, but where is your fiancée." Murray said, "We're looking for her now. I'm sure she has some poor soul trapped in some time loop paradox or a debate over whether Schrödinger's cat is dead or alive. If we find her, we'll bail out the guy and try to find you, until then, cheers."

Just as they were finally going back in the restaurant, they heard very loud music coming from the parking lot, or should I say the car show. It was live music. Ratzi looked over and saw his dad and mom sitting on a porch swing just as happy as could be. He looked at Carole and she was already looking at him. They looked back at Ratzi's parents and there was just a fusion of loving understanding. Ratzi's mother said, "You're starving, get something good to eat, you're going to be married in two hours."

Inside, Robert and Rhonda took the couple to a private dining room. They didn't have to ask. Their favorite dishes were on the table already. Ratzi looked down at the food and almost cried. He said, "What a host. What a friend you are taking care of me all these years. Really, we're just Robby and Ratzi. I mean in here, we're just those same two guys that went to school together and worked hard and made the big time." Carole said, "We love you both, and we love the Homestead. Thank you." Robert said back, "Well Mr. and Mrs. Rige, we love you too, but bear in mind, you are paying for this so what we're doing here ain't entirely love." Carole said to Rhonda, "Rhonda, I know you would never do anything indiscrete in front of even us, but when you get this jackass alone would you ..... well, you know." Rhonda turned to Robert and said, "Sentiment Rob, Sentiment." The three of them hugged each other for a long time. Finally Ratzi said, "Excuse me, I'm starving."

After they had their lunch they retreated separately to dress for the ceremony. When they came out, the restaurant was quiet. Everybody was assembled. The ceremony wasn't some picture perfect, over rehearsed quasi funeral. It was light and fun, with jokes being told, and self-deprecating humor done with sincere affection. The ceremony was presided by Aimee Tzu who was there at the very beginning trying to get a foothold in politics and was now one of the State's Senators. She said in an interview that she had never been more proud of her duties as when she had the honor of pronouncing Carole Kozlowski and Orazio Rige man and wife.

The happy couple ran out of the front door of the Homestead and jumped into an antique Limo to be whisked off to Yachats for their first night together as husband and wife. They would be back the following afternoon for the reception if anyone was still alive after the party that would go on that night. Only the Blacks knew that the honeymoon was going to be in Yachats, they had told no one. They had a beautiful house there that no one really knew about. It was on twenty two acres and had some real nice beach front. Ratzi and Carole had never been there. When the chauffeur dropped them off, the silence was luxurious. There were plenty of provisions, enough for probably a month. Orazio just opened a bottle of Chardonnay and poured a glass for his wife and himself. She took her glass and held it up. They looked into each other's eyes and Carole said, "We did it." Orazio said, "Yes, we're married." Carole said, "No, we changed the world."

Chapter Nineteen

Bona Pax Ordinis

Orazio Rige and countless others did do it. They changed the world and survived it. The wedding was as much a celebration of that as it was a celebration of the love that Carole and Ratzi shared.

When the limo came back for them, this time the Toad Limo, they felt the full impact of what had happened over the previous eight years. Orazio, Ratzi for those who loved him, was all out of ambition. He really wanted probably four kids to raise along with his love, the most people-person he could even imagine. He pictured opening a Charter School so that it would be ready for when his children were. He would provide a great building and hire wonderful teachers. Koz would pick them and they would be paid well. He was so eager. Koz too was picturing nothing but the same. They held hands during the ride.

Back at the Homestead the party was in full swing. There was a great band playing out in the parking lot and Carole knew what she heard. She said, "Orazio, we gotta go see the band first before we go back inside." Ratzi said, "Orazio?" The limo driver responded to Carole by driving them through the parking lot to as close to the band as he could get. He jumped out and opened the door for his passengers. As they stepped out he said, "Watch the Wolf" and gave them a big knowing grin. Ratzi asked, "What did he mean by that?" Carole said, "Watch the Wolf Ratzi, you're finally going to hear Oscar's band."

Orazio Rige couldn't believe his eyes. It was the guys who built the Toad, and there at the drums, was Oscar

Rodriguez kicking his ass again, rockin' out like the star that he was, and everybody else; wow, the Mexican hot-rodders from Los Angeles playing at his wedding just for the fun of it. Damn Oscar, honoring him again.

Oscar saw Mr. Rige coming up in the limo. He signaled the band. They finished the song they were playing and Oscar spoke into the microphone, this one's for you *jefe*. The band started up again and only in a few moments the drum solo started. Oscar was going crazy at the drums. Carole was smiling ear to ear. Ratzi looked at her. He had the feeling he was not in on something. Leonardo, the guy standing next to him was the man who had painted his copper colored car. Ratzi asked him, "My wife is smiling kinda funny, do you know the name of this song?" Leonardo just looked at him, shrugged, and said, "Toad!"

*****

The reception was lunch at two o'clock. The band had stopped and Ratzi thanked Oscar and the rest of the band for honoring him. Oscar told him that they were honoring Bobby Diez too. He was killed in the cyber-control war and Lucas took it hard. Ratzi told Oscar that he had talked to Lucas the day before, but Lucas said nothing of it. Oscar said that if he had told you that news on your wedding day, his mother would've slapped the shit out of him.

As Ratzi and Carole turned to go back inside the Homestead, Donna and Marla Black were standing there. They were smiling funny too.

Donna: How'd you like the house, kids?

Carole: We love it. We can't wait to get back there and really get comfortable. You know, see all the rooms and explore the grounds.

Marla: You'll have all the time you need for that. That place is our wedding gift to you. We figured it was a great place to raise kids, and we know that's your next passion so .....

Ratzi: No, you can't do that. It's too much. We both have houses. We .....

Carole: Darling, they need you to say thank you. Just say it.

Orazio Rige grabbed the three women and hugged them all. He said, "I think we have too much money." Donna said back, "I don't know how, I certainly never tried to make any." Orazio smiled as he said, "We're making a lot more than money. We're making wealth for the whole nation, and a government that doesn't waste it. People all over the world will see. America will be the shining city on the hill again."

Donna Black looked back and saw that there were a thousand people waiting to see Ratzi and Carole. She called out to them, "Let's take it inside everybody." She looked at Carole and asked, "Mrs. Rige?" Carole said back, "That name is a dream-come-true. Ratzi and Carole Rige, I couldn't love it more."

The crowd parted and "The Riges" paraded across the still dazzling parking lot car show and into Robert and Rhonda's Homestead. The place simply wasn't built to handle the crowd that showed up. Cars were parked along the drive, all the way out to the road.

The couple sat at their table and the reception started. Ratzi's brother Vito asked everybody to raise their glass and he said, "My brother wants you all to drink to each other, he loves you all. Please turn to the person next to you and say, we'll do it together, we'll do it for love." Next Matty raised his glass. He said, "My definition of a friend is someone who accepts you as you are, and invites you to grow. I'm ex-army. If you know that Orazio and Carole are my best friends, and maybe yours, give me a good U.S. Army Hooah." The crowd yelled Hooah, and Matty said, "I can't hear you." and crowd yelled again, this time laughing as Matty was laughing himself.

As the people all started to sit down, the first couple to approach the Riges was Deanna Segal and her Husband Lloyd. She said, "We'll do it together, we'll do it for love," and Orazio asked, "Well Della, have I met your standard?" She said back, "Yes Ratzi Rige, the day you married Carole Kozlowski." Carole began to cry.

The people filed by. Vito and Matty took shifts keeping them moving. After an hour, it looked like it was never going to end so Vito signaled the band to start and as the people began to dance. Ratzi and Carole slipped out through of all places, the kitchen. Out back, Oscar and Xiomara had Ratzi's copper colored Toad waiting for him. The security guys from Rainforest had cleared an exit, you know, a fire lane, for the clean getaway. Carole kissed Xiomara and jumped behind the wheel. She looked up with a look on her face that asked, "What?" Oscar looked at Ratzi with a little look of panic. Mr. Rige cleared his throat, and Carole slid over on the bench seat as Orazio Rige took his seat. They looked up at Oscar and Xiomara and caught them kissing. Ratzi closed the door and slipped silently away.

*****

The honeymoon went long, but eventually both Carole and Orazio returned to work. Deanna had done a great job of handling the business of Rige Coos Bay, but there were people waiting to talk with the boss.

Scott Platt, Jimmy Capasso and Johnny Bencivene politely gave Mr. Rige time to get reacquainted with his desk, and showed up at his office around ten. They brought him up to speed on how they were running the world. Very few secrets could be kept from them by any nation. The only way real cyber secrecy could be maintained was to have completely closed systems. You could have a computer on your desk for common search and social media, but for work, you could not be online at all ever. Every keystroke, every phone message was kept somewhere unless it "didn't happen." Even personal visits were hard to keep clandestine with the amount of cameras that were all over every building and up and down every street. Of all the "Big Brothers" Rainforest had become the biggest.

Orazio was happy to hear this for his friends, but sad to hear it for the world. He had a taste of retirement in the country, but was beginning to understand that there was no "country" any more. The children he would raise would never know the romantic feeling of happily lost on an old country road. They'd be satellite connected no matter where they went, and even worse, through the responsibility of love, Rainforest would never let them out of view. He thought, at what cost protection? That image of the individual freedom of alone on the frontier was appealing to him. There was no word for this feeling, and now it seemed, there would be no sensation of it either. It was almost as if there was an evolutionary loss of an entire emotion. Orazio felt the loss.

*****

Orazio was surprised to see that the next person to visit him was Lucas Vasquez. Orazio welcomed him warmly and invited him to eat. Lucas said, "I'm not really hungry." Orazio said, "It's pizza," and Lucas said back, "Well, maybe a slice." He ended up eating three.

As they ate, he told Orazio that in addition to lift off and landing with robotic vehicles, they had resolved the radiation problem with electromagnetic fields. Now it was possible to send a person up safely, though there was no point in it. A man wouldn't be functional in space because of the human need for gravity. They needed to create a centrifuge large enough to create centrifugal artificial gravity without the problem of the Coriolis Effect. The centrifuge would have to be miles long. The amount of space mining to accomplish this would take time. It would need to be done with robotic construction. Once the software and hardware was written and constructed, the actual work would be automatic, but the project was inestimable in scope. It would be "learn by doing," and would need a serious commitment because anything but completion would be nothing but a waste of time and money.

Orazio asked why Murray Atkins didn't come with this proposal. Lucas told him that Murray didn't feel that he had enough answers to your potential questions yet. He wanted to be further along on the research and development of the project. He told Orazio that the truth was Murray didn't even know about the meeting we're having.

Orazio looked deeply at Lucas, and wished he had Carole there. He was trying to read him as Carole would have. Lucas saw this. He was trying to mind read too. Finally he said, "You suspect that I am imposing on you depending on your friendship with my father. I am not." Orazio was speechless. The thought had entered his mind. Lucas said, "The way my father thinks of you is the reason I am here. Murray doesn't have my insight into your courage. He thinks of you as rich. Dad thinks of you as a street fighter who just happened to make the right moves and won the right battles. Murray is trapped in the play for pay, financial result paradigm. I think you and I are pioneers. I come to you in that spirit, not in a spirit of imposition on your relationship with my dad, but to honor that relationship by giving you yet another chance to kick ass. I didn't come here to rob your bank. I came here to establish my own relationship with you, the fucking dude my dad always described you as, the fucking dude that I believe you are."

Orazio said, "You're quite a young man Lucas Vasquez. I'm sorry about your loss of Bobby Diez. I know that he engaged that brain of yours and in a special way, expanded your life worth living into new frontiers. I've been thinking a lot about that lately."

Lucas: He never treated me like a kid. He treated me like an equal. If anything I treated him like a kid. He was to me, a playmate. We played together. I thought nothing of how special he was. Now I know. I wish I could work with him now that I do work, and not just play.

Orazio: Lucas, always just play. Isn't what you do now still your game?

Lucas: No, Mr. Rige. What I do now is work, because people depend on me. I have responsibility, so no, its work, and not just some game.

Orazio: As I said, you're quit a man and you're right about me, I will finance your work. Did your father tell you I would?

Lucas: He doesn't know I'm here.

Orazio just looked at him, the next generation of talent coming from a father and mother of extraordinary depth of ethics, morals, talent and class. He and Carole would think of Jando and Lola as they raised their own children. He was as well put together as one of his father and mother's beautiful cars; flawless. He said, "So why don't you go ahead and tell me what we need in space."

Lucas: Well, it all starts with a giant iron ball. The cool thing is always that in a weightless environment, big mass is easy to move around. The big iron ball is to make the huge electromagnet that will set up artificial Van Allen Belts. That's for radiation protection.

Next, you begin to build the habitat. So that gravity is straight down and not in an arc, you need to have the centrifuge miles long. You want the Coriolis deflection of fall or lean to be imperceptible. On Earth it's not a problem because we get our down force from gravity. For us, the down force will be from centrifugal force. We as organisms still need the downforce, however we get it. We just don't want to have it in an arc. It makes baseball too weird.

So we have the big magnet core, and we have the big arm with the habitat on it and to balance the habitat arm, we need a counter weight. So we build that in conjunction with the habitat arm. We start small but constantly add. The development speed is okay because we are learning a million things as the project develops. Once we get a start where people can survive there, physical growth will be mostly

193

robotic, so mostly automatic. In other words, as the mining vehicles bring more stuff, the construction robots will refine it and add it to our supply of resources. The idea is to be completely independent from Earth.

Orazio: Wait 'til you tell Murray about this meeting huh?

Lucas: He's a good man Mr. Rige, just a little timid about money. I think he was poor in college, and has that frugal bent. I never knew poverty, even when we were poor. Plus, he's not family the way we are.

Orazio: Is he capable of overseeing a project of this magnitude?

Lucas: That's a great question. We're going to grow into this project, and nothing like this has been done by any of us. There's potential for challenges, but we've got a good team so I'll say yes for now, and if there are any problems, I'll let you know at the first sign. We can't fool around with this, it's really important.

Orazio: You know Lucas, I'm so impressed with this that I'm going to oversee it myself. I usually have an accountant executive-direct funding, but I want you to come to me directly for money. I do this because I want to learn, and so much of my other responsibilities are covered by others, kinda whether I like it or not. I don't see myself as hands-on in any way, but I do want to be eyes-on.

Lucas: Yeah, I want you to too.

Orazio: Okay then, take off. Get it?

Lucas: Goofy.

Orazio: Well, it's just not a great meeting if it doesn't end silly so report back soon and good luck.

Lucas: Thank you Mr. Rige. You can bet I'll see you soon.

That evening Oscar Rodriguez called Orazio to thank him for supporting Jando's son. Orazio wasn't surprised. He joked that he now had a whole new generations of the family working with him, and that maybe if his wedding tackle was working, they always would. Oscar said it would be a blessing if that was to happen. Orazio agreed and asked him if he and his wife would like to come down to the beach house for a few days for a change of scenery. After talking with his wife, he said that they would love to, in the eight years they worked together; they had never just kicked back and did nothing. It was time to get together and listen to a few old records or watch a few old movies.

That weekend they showed up. Xiomara did the driving in her Chevelle. Ratzi said, "I can't believe that you don't use a Toad." Oscar said back, "We do, but this is vacation and so Xiomara takes her show car to make it extra special. Ratzi looked at her and asked, "You really love this car don't you?" She smiled back and said, "Why do you think I married this *matón*." Carole came out of the house to greet her friends and Xiomara said, "Oh my God, congratulations." Both men looked at their ladies and they looked back. "I'm pregnant," Carole said.

A few months later, Sammy Zane got wind of Carole and Ratzi's upcoming blessing. Naturally, every medical exam had been done, and Carole was about a month away from delivering a baby boy. Sammy Zane sat down with them. He told them that his practice of DNA therapy was working with great success and zero danger to his clients. What he recommended was, let him take the DNA samples and store them. The baby most likely would not need any kind of medical intervention for maybe decades, but it would be good to have the samples in case and when he ever did. By the time he did need them, a vast amount of experience would be behind him and the safety factor which he felt was perfect now would be reinforced far more. Both parents agreed. Take the samples, there's no harm in that, but Mr. Rige insisted that he be able to store the samples himself. He didn't want his family's DNA up for weird cloning experiments or any such medical exploration in the future. Dr. Zane agreed.

*****

Three years passed, and Carole and her husband had a boy, a girl and another one in the oven. Their life was quiet and secure. Their businesses were running themselves and the new more accountable government was allowing the people to thrive. America was strong. Family values were coming back because there was no longer room for subversive incursion. The Toad was everywhere. It had been just as Oscar had said. The American car culture had returned, especially because of the zero emission cheap fuel. The Toad was sometime unrecognizable, that's how crazy the customizers went.

The helium battery made America rich. It was a bigger export than any other item in the world except food. The Space Force turned out to be the other savior of the world. Arms buildups were impractical. The Space Force just wouldn't allow it. Rainforest was on top of everything worldwide. There was so much surveillance that the only thing that made sense for anybody was to "do the right thing." Much more energy was being put toward creation than destruction. It was a renaissance, a rebirth of civilization after a savage era.

Orazio's own Space research company was also making its strides. Dana Morea, you know, Mrs. Earth, was fascinated with it. She wanted in badly, and wasn't ashamed to marry Mitch Roggenbuck to get there. At least, that's what everybody said. She was exasperated that everybody wanted to waste the real estate of the centrifugal counterweight. She wanted to farm it. She pointed out that it didn't have to be habitable for humans, just for agriculture. She became obsessed with getting bacteria up there. There was a programmer who was in love with Dana's sister, and she coerced him into writing the program for transforming the massive inert ball of material in the counterweight into a prairie. All she wanted was organic matter to accumulate, something about a peat base. It was done.

As the station grew in size, people started to migrate there. People from Dr. Zane's company saw a future in space. Programmers from Rainforest did too. Even a few AI robotic professionals from Lana's Oregasm Company found an important place. The headhunting began. Very select people were invited to join the elite group of off-worlders. Brothers Space Enterprise was very independent and secretive about their technology. They did not work for profit. They kept themselves separate from the rest of the world in that way, Orazio Rige allowed it and the Black sisters defended it. Even Rainforest was obligated by some unknown agreement to protect it. It just was not available to the public.

The station was called *"Away"* by those going there. It had accumulated over a thousand people and had a habitable surface area of about five hundred square miles. From the center stanchion arm, you would be able to see more than twelve miles in all directions. Water and air were recirculating in an ecosystem. They were growing their own food. Both habitable platforms were more than six miles from the center magnet protecting them from radiation. It was clear that the beginning of two more centrifugal spokes were being formed. The mining and construction robots were relentless. *Away,* which was in synchronous orbit above the Brothers Space Enterprise launch base was suddenly moved another hundred miles from the Earth. It was the final test.

At that time, the announcement was made.

We, the people of the *Away* project are indeed ready to go away. We intend to go to the asteroid belt where mining is greater and more local. When we have built our colony to sufficient size, we will head to the edge of the solar system. We will do any additional mining if necessary in the Kuiper Belt before exploring the outer edge of our Star's solar wind's influence on space. If leaving the solar system is possible, we will inform you. If it is possible, we may well leave you forever.

Our goal is to explore space as pure inhabitants of it, not as dependent visitors from Earth. We have a very clean and pure society with which to start. We are not governed by the prejudices that come from a planetary past. Each one of us has been picked by group consensus. We are all equal in that we are all scientists with an above average intelligence quotient. We are one generation away from children who have no memory of planetary life and will find the idea of that life with its diseases, pestilence, weather and crime abhorrent. There will be no race or religious division, as we have no diversity with the problems that brings. There will be no poverty, mal-nutrition or ignorance. We are all Philosophers first, lovers of knowledge. We embark on a bold experiment. We are you, we

are human, so wish us well if you have it in you. If not, well
….. That's on you.

Your world is in relatively good order thanks to our visionary benefactor. We wish you well and hope you can keep it that way. Always remember your past and rejoice in the positive change of trajectory his philosophy has provided. He had money. What he did, he did because he loves you.

We leave our equipment behind and plenty of expertise in how to use it. That is our gift to you. Once again, we hope you use it wisely.

We will always love our Mother Earth, but are finally able to cut her apron strings.

We may return, anything is possible, but probably not.

For those of you who love the beautiful planet you were born on and can't imagine why anyone would leave it, we understand. Count your blessings that you are still here. Please try to understand us. We must do what our nature demands. We have the bold confidence and courage of natural explorers. We understand you, and hope that you understand us. We love you all.

Murray Atkins closed the door on his ship to make his final departure. There weren't many cameras at the unannounced event. Lucas Vasquez, who could just never leave his family, was there with his camera to catch the words painted over the door.

Bona Pax Ordinis

Prosperity Peace Order

Murray was greeted at *Away* with wild applause. The electromagnetic envelope was created and *Away* began to move toward the asteroid belt. He saw Mitch Roggenbuck and Dana Morea standing there with something in their hand. He asked, "What is that?" Mitch and Dana looked at each other and then back at Murray. Mitch said, "Rod Rodriguez gave us this before we took off as his gift to us." Okay Murray said, "But what is it."

The two looked at each other again and Dana said,

"You know Rod. It's the Hydrogen Battery."